Cate maneuvered into the parking lot adjacent to the main road, jumped out of her car, and headed for the employee golf carts used as a means to get around the grounds. Taking the first available, she hurled the little cart in the direction of Guest Services. Whizzing past beachgoers sporting island T-shirts, she spied customers coming out of Novel Ideas, the island's long-standing, secondhand bookstore.

Slowing at the curve in front of Island Scoop, Cate wished for a cool treat to reward her sweet tooth. The strong aroma of steaming coffee alerted her to a few visitors coming out of The Wise Owl, sipping cups of morning brew. Blocking her view, they strolled along the path toward the boardwalk. Their telltale bronzed skin and relaxed demeanor signaled the end of their stay. Cate couldn't blame them for wanting to linger, but she was in a hurry.

When they finally set out, she zipped her cart into the only open parking spot. Cate entered the building and scooted by the buzzing groups now congregating in front of the shiny Guest Services counter, careful not to make eye contact. She shifted her belongings to cover up her navy polo embroidered with the Gull Island insignia to ward off unwanted conversation until she could get settled and prepared to offer assistance.

Serendipity by the Sea

by

Jennifer Vido

The Gull Island Series

Serendipity by the Sea

COPYRIGHT © 2022 by Jennifer Vido

Cover Art by *Kristian Norris*

The Wild Rose Press, Inc.
PO Box 708
Adams Basin, NY 14410-0708
Visit us at www.thewildrosepress.com

Publishing History
First Edition, 2023
Trade Paperback ISBN 978-1-5092-4785-1
Digital ISBN 978-1-5092-4786-8

The Gull Island Series
Published in the United States of America

Dedication

For Vicki Ireland and Laurie Vido, my Fripp Island
sisters.
And for Sally LeSage, my forever friend.

Acknowledgements

The inspiration for this novel came from a family vacation to Fripp Island, South Carolina. Little did I know at the time how this beautiful barrier island would set in motion the idea for a sweet romance series.

Thank you to my editor, Leanne Morgena, for her invaluable insight and knowledge during the editing process.

Thank you to Ann-Marie Nieves of Get Red PR for getting this book into the hands of readers.

Thank you to Bree Greene and Malia Schreiber of Millennial Marketing for their social media expertise.

My big dream became a reality because I am surrounded by love and encouragement from the Plisky & Vido families and my supportive friends.

I am appreciative to my early readers who generously offered their time and provided input. In particular, I'd like to thank Liz Durbin, Terri Garland, and Nikki Horton for welcoming Cate and Knox into their hearts.

Thank you to Sally LeSage for loving Gull Island and shrimp boats as much as I do. The late nights, numerous rewrites, and scrutinizing over sentences was worth it.

Thank you to the Fripp Island crew—Vicki, Laurie, Frank, Will, and Emily—who contributed each in their own way. I can't wait for our next adventure.

And finally, to Durbin, Henry, and Sam—your unwavering support and love guides my literary career. I love you with all my heart.

Chapter One

Cate Ainsworth gritted her teeth, thumbs drumming time on the steering wheel, while a long line of cars backed up on the drawbridge to Gull Island. Like the summer visitors anxious to arrive at their destination in South Carolina, Cate could only wait out the clanking steel structure rising at a sharp angle, making way for a rickety shrimp boat to chug forward through the Intracoastal Waterway. Breathing in the briny sea air, she glanced at her dashboard clock, the minutes ticking by, realizing she should've left home earlier. At a complete standstill, she flicked on the radio to take her mind off being late to work, again. Her shift already began at Guest Services; yet here she was, stuck on the bridge.

A buzz vibrating from her bag on the passenger's seat vied for her attention. As the car idled, she rummaged through it for the source. Setting the phone in the hands-free holder, she hesitated to answer at the sight of Eliza Brown's name on the caller ID. Not only was Eliza her coworker, but she also was her best friend. They attended school together in Beaufort and spent summers on the island, hanging out at Cate's grandmother's cottage. Cate hated to let her friend down. The overwhelmed voice she'd encounter on the other end was entirely on her.

"Are you running late again?" Eliza's high-pitched

voice echoed in the car.

Cate winced, disappointed she'd left Eliza to open by herself.

The traffic on Gull Island was heavier in the summer, something she was well aware of but rarely took into consideration when driving to work from Beaufort. Off-season, the average commute time from the city to the island was forty minutes. Moving into the beach cottage while her grammy, as family and friends lovingly referred to her, was away would help alleviate the common occurrence, or at least that's what she was telling herself. Time would tell, pun intended. "If it weren't for the drawbridge being up, I would have been on time," Cate said, feebly, craning her neck to view the traffic jam.

"No need to explain for my benefit," Eliza countered. "I'm the only one here."

"I'll be there soon. Traffic's moving." Cate bit her thumbnail, feeling awful for leaving Eliza to handle everything this morning. Being late on check-in day meant one thing—disgruntled guests.

As Cate approached the island, she maneuvered her car into the right lane for locals, leaving the never-ending line of visitors needing a guest pass for island parking to the left. The guard on duty waved her on, much appreciated in her present circumstances.

Maneuvering into the parking lot adjacent to the main road, Cate jumped out of her car and headed for the employee golf carts used as a means to get around the grounds. Taking the first available, she hurled the little cart in the direction of Guest Services. Whizzing past beachgoers sporting island T-shirts, she spied customers coming out of Novel Ideas, the island's long-standing, secondhand bookstore. Slowing at the curve in front of Island Scoop, Cate wished for a cool treat to reward her sweet tooth. The strong aroma of steaming coffee alerted her to a few visitors coming out of The Wise Owl, sipping cups of morning brew. Blocking her view, they strolled along the path toward the boardwalk. Their telltale bronzed skin and relaxed demeanor signaled the end of their stay. Cate couldn't blame them for wanting to linger, but she was in a hurry.

When they finally set out, she zipped her cart into the only open parking spot. Cate entered the building and scooted by the buzzing groups now congregating in front of the shiny Guest Services counter, careful not to make eye contact. She shifted her belongings to cover up her navy polo embroidered with the Gull Island insignia to ward off unwanted conversation until she could get settled and prepared to offer assistance.

Cate spotted the platinum blonde hair of her five-foot-two best friend peering from behind the check-in desk, perched high upon a stool, pounding on the computer and shoving room keys into paper folders amid the sound of the temperamental printer humming.

"Full house today," Eliza announced, flashing teeth through her fixed smile.

"Give me a minute," she mouthed. Cate rushed toward the back of the office to stash her belongings. In the break room, she scanned the white wicker baskets with navy lettering lining the shelf, full of random stuff like office supplies and extra island maps. Grabbing her mandatory name tag, she slapped it on, tossed in her belongings, then darted back out front to help Eliza greet the arriving guests.

While the crowds were large, she had one thing going for her. Early on, Cate learned on the job that weather dictated the mood of the visitors. Sunny skies and cool breezes drew smiles and laughter. Rainy days with gusty winds guaranteed long faces and antsy children in need of supervision. The day's temperature registered in the low 80s, unseasonably mild for June, and ideal beach weather for locals and tourists alike. Cate wagered her morning shift would be smooth sailing if the weather held.

Cate hustled to her spot alongside Eliza, beaming in welcome for the clients, while her stomach clenched with guilt for leaving her friend to handle this. "My wife and I were *tawlking* about our stay. We're sad to be leaving the Lowcountry hospitality behind," said Frank Martini, a tall, broad man with a thick Northern accent. "It'll be snowing in upstate New York in no time." A frequent visitor to the island, he handed his credit card to Cate.

"On the bright side, you now have another vacation to plan," Cate replied. "I've booked you in your favorite beach cottage for the same two weeks next June."

"Perfect," Frank answered with a satisfied smile.

Cate swiped the credit card and leaned down to catch the receipt from the printer. "And you're all set." She handed him the paperwork and his card. "See you next year."

When the morning rush died down, Cate flopped onto the textured white sofa, trailing her hand along the soft fabric. She took full advantage of the empty room.

Eliza followed her lead and lounged on the opposite end of the couch.

"Sorry I was late *again*. Not even bothering to make up an excuse. I have none. Plus, I missed your text last night. I'm a hot mess." Cate rolled her shoulders and finally caught a breath.

"Let me guess," replied Eliza. "Nose stuck in a novel?" Her friend grinned.

Cate nibbled on her nail. She needed to get out and enjoy herself, but spending time on Gull Island without Grammy would be an adjustment.

"You say you need to make friends and be social, but you'll never meet people if all you do is stay home," Eliza cautioned. "You missed the most amazing sunset on Beach Head Point. *And,* lots of people our age."

"I'm sorry I didn't go. In my defense, my car is loaded with stuff," she rationalized. "I'm finally moving into Grammy's beach cottage today after work so I'll be busy. But the good news is my commute won't be an issue anymore." She lifted her fists above her head in celebration.

"Here's hoping." Eliza gave a slight nod, rolling her eyes skyward.

"Want to grab a bite at The Shack later?" Cate offered. The Seaside Shack, nicknamed The Shack by the locals, was one of Eliza's favorite spots. "Jackson works the swing shift." An excellent excuse to keep tabs on her younger brother.

"Absolutely." Eliza fiddled with her name tag, hanging askew on her navy uniform polo.

The door chimes interrupted their slight reprieve.

"I'll race you to the front desk." Eliza scrambled from her seated position.

"You're on." Cate leaped to her feet.

The afternoon rush lasted for hours. The pair worked as a team handing out rental keys, maps of the island, and lists of activities aimed to keep the summer tourists entertained. They could easily recite the spiel in their sleep, having worked together for three years.

Cate loved the small-town feel of Gull Island, despite its being a vacation destination. On her way into the office, she enjoyed seeing the old timers congregating at the local post office in the morning for newsy tidbits. The highlight of her day was chatting with Ol' Man Henry, who dropped by every afternoon at two on the dot with freshly baked treats, like chocolate chip cookies or frosted cupcakes. He was the keeper of the important goings-on.

Bait & Switch, the no-frills tackle shop located at the inlet, was owned by Charlie Price, a close family friend. The history of the place always captivated her. A focal point of the island, the former Coast Guard Station consisted of two floors and an observation post. Decommissioned and auctioned off in the early '90s, Charlie snatched it up.

Tourists often popped in for sundries after picking up their vacation golf carts at the rental shop across the way. Locals snatched up the fresh catch from the fishermen who docked their boats at the nearby slips.

The first floor contained overpriced suntan lotion, last-minute pantry items, and island T-shirts in bright colors. A makeshift grill served basic fare, like tasty breakfast sandwiches made with farm fresh eggs and pork sausage and gooey grilled ham and cheeses. The Bait & Switch shop also served as the designated late check-in spot for tourists entering the island, starting at five o'clock, which was posted on a sign on Guest

Services' door.

"Closing time," announced Cate. "I'll drop off the remaining welcome packages at Bait & Switch on my way. Meet you at The Shack?"

Eliza flipped over the front door sign to *Closed*. "That works. I'll stop by my house and change first. Do you mind if I ask Will to join us if he's home?"

Friends with Eliza's boyfriend since childhood, she reasoned. "The more, the merrier." She needed to force herself to be social. *Time to get on with her life*.

****

Knox Price drove along the coastal highway, breathing in the familiar salty air through the open window of his rented Chevy pickup truck, his hair blowing across his forehead. As a native of South Carolina, he grew up in Beaufort and spent his summers on the Gull Island shore for as long as he could remember.

Early on, Knox planned to leave sleepy Beaufort, the laid-back seaside town he used to call home, to pursue a fast-paced marketing job in New York City. At his father's urging, he attended an elite college in New England where worldly Northerners found his deep Southern drawl fascinating. He still remembered the night his father, Kevin, sat him down.

"Son, there's more out there than this little town. You've got a lot of livin' to do. Go make something of yourself."

Knox did just that. He worked hard at school, graduating with honors and landing a six-figure job on Madison Avenue. But, sitting behind a desk as a marketing analyst did not satisfy his natural inclination to be outdoors, nor did it fill the emptiness inside.

Although photography had long been a hobby, he honed his skills and submitted his work to travel magazines. He told his best friend that he'd flood the in-box of every acquiring editor until someone said "yes." Slowly, the offers poured in, which fueled his desire for more. He transformed his pipedream into a budding and lucrative career as a freelance nature photographer.

Returning to Gull Island flooded him with mixed emotions. He hadn't set eyes on the familiar bridge in a long time. As soon as Knox graduated from college, his parents packed up and relocated closer to his mom's family in upstate New York. So, when his dad left him a voicemail saying Knox's favorite uncle Charlie was having surgery and could use a helping hand, Knox sensed a strong need to rush to the island.

In his younger years, his parents worked long hours; his mother was a real estate agent, and his father was a computer analyst. Knox spent many summers following his uncle around the marina and working in the store. His uncle made him feel important, wanted…worthy, filling the gap when his parents were occupied with making a living.

Knox's uncle was a favorite among the summer visitors. As the owner of Bait & Switch, he interacted with nearly everyone on the island, locals and tourists alike. His knowledge of the island knew no bounds. Being one with nature, the man was privy to the best fishing spots and could locate dolphins and sea turtles with ease. His innate love of nature rubbed off on Knox, fueling his interest in untamed landscapes.

Sitting high in his truck, Knox cruised along the main road through traffic onto Gull Island, sneaking glimpses of native island birds like snowy white egrets and great blue herons swooping in and out of his sightline. Not much changed. Brightly colored houses with placards displaying catchy, beach-themed names welcomed him home. Mother Nature was kind to the island. Over the years, hurricanes came and went, but none left lasting damage to the coastline.

Knox drifted through each section of cottages, bungalows, and villas, paying mind to distracted visitors sightseeing on bicycles. When Bait & Switch finally loomed in the distance, he eased up on the gas pedal and coasted around the curve.

Guests gathered outside the door of the golf cart rental office situated diagonally across from his uncle's business. Only two people were permitted inside at a time, a rule strictly enforced by the staff. Sweat gathered on the brows of customers waiting to enter the air-conditioned oasis. The sight jogged his memory of his childhood self, wanting to cut the cart line to get to the beach faster. Even now, the sound of the surf called his name.

Instead of fighting for a parking space out front, Knox veered to the rear of the building where he found his uncle's silver truck parked in the reserved handicapped space. He eased into an adjacent spot and killed the engine. Knox hesitated for a moment, steeling himself to face what might lie ahead. Grabbing his keys, he slid out of the pickup and headed inside.

The commotion of the store produced a smile despite his trepidation. Years passed, but his uncle's thriving business remained the same. Fidgety kids placed their fingers on whatever was in reach, while the adults did their best to grab what was necessary in a hurry.

"Don't just stand there, son. Make yourself useful," a growly voice called from behind the crowded counter.

Seeing his tall, lanky uncle in his element eased the tension in his shoulders. His uncle's present health condition had done little to slow him down. "Yes, sir." Knox slipped behind a group of teens to squeeze into position. The checkout line snaked around the aisles, leaving little wiggle room for guests.

"You're okay with the, umm, cash register?" Uncle Charlie spoke in his familiar raspy drawl.

Knox eyed the under-the-counter drawer with dividers ajar, stuffed with cash collected. Years ago, he surprised Charlie with a key-punch box register hoping to modernize the store. There it sat barely used, wedged at the far end of the counter collecting dust. The ATM machine tucked in the back corner was the only modern concession his uncle made. "I got you." He offered a quick fist jab to his uncle, making light of the fact that he was worried about him.

Side by side, they worked in tandem with Knox handling the cash and his uncle making small talk with the customers. The constant noise and influx of people left little time for catching up, and Knox could feel the elephant in the room getting bigger. Not trusting his level of sensitivity, he mulled over the best approach as to when to ask about his uncle's health issues.

With suppertime quickly approaching, the crowd dwindled. Summer guests regrouped at their rental homes to wash off sand, apply aloe to their sunburnt skin, and dress in their most acceptable beach casual wear for dinner. Many would return later to admire the picturesque sunset at Beach Head Point.

Meanwhile, Knox and Uncle Charlie used the break in the action to restock the shelves for the next day. The store remained open until ten o'clock for late arrivals and last-minute must-haves.

Uncle Charlie focused on the task at hand, moving about the store at a slow and steady pace.

Like clockwork, a stray calico cat stopped by in the alley for a dinnertime snack of scraps. With the back door ajar, its persistent mewing echoed inside the building.

Delighted the island felines still hung around, Knox stepped outside. He stroked the calico's head as he lumped bits of chicken from the scrap bucket into the small bowl.

"I'm taking the trash to the dumpster," Charlie said. "While I'm gone, go ahead and count the till. Put those college smarts to use."

"Yes, sir."

Uncle Charlie grabbed two overstuffed, green trash bags in his weathered hands. "When you finish, round up the recyclables, will ya?" Not waiting for a response, he exited through the rear door.

Knox couldn't help but notice his uneven gait and hunched shoulders. Taking out the cash drawer, Knox placed it on the counter. He withdrew a wad of bills, arranged them neatly in stacks by denomination, and deposited the coins on the side to keep them separate. In doing so, some change rolled off the counter, clattering to the floorboards. Startled by the jingling of the door, Knox squatted beneath it to retrieve them. "What'd you do, sprint?" he shouted.

No one answered. Knox chalked it up to Charlie being hard of hearing and continued feeling around for the scattered coins. The man's reluctance to admit his need for hearing aids was well-known among family and locals. Rather than badger Charlie to get his hearing checked, his family and friends simply chose to raise their volume when speaking to him.

"Hello?" a soft Southern accent broke the silence.

Knox cocked his ear to get a better listen. The voice most certainly didn't belong to his uncle.

"Anyone here?" the woman spoke a little louder.

Knox bit his bottom lip. The *tap-tap-tap* of athletic footsteps fast approached. He crouched lower, willing to stay hidden just a bit longer until he could get his bearings. When the steps halted, he drew in a deep breath of air, hinted with a faint smell of jasmine, and emerged.

"Oh," Cate squealed. "Knox." Her voice lifted an octave. "What are you doing hiding behind there? You nearly scared me to death."

"Sorry," was all he could get out. The shock of seeing his former girlfriend's radiant face and shimmering, light-brown hair sucked the wind right out of his lungs. A slight twinge of excitement shot through him. A glance at Cate's work polo along with the stack of blue envelopes in her hand told him all he needed to know. "Dropping off the welcome packages for the late arrivals?"

Cate slid them across the counter. "Quite a few. Two sets of keys are inside each one. If the guests need more, please send them over to the office in the morning. We'll be happy to provide them. The golf cart rental agreements are included in the paperwork, too. If they don't pick up the carts before five tomorrow evening, they'll be out of luck. From what I understand, the rental shop has a waiting list."

"That's it?"

"The rest is self-explanatory," she called over her shoulder on her way toward the exit. "I highlighted the route to each rental on the enclosed maps, so they shouldn't have trouble finding them at dusk or dark. The island isn't that big, or have you forgotten your way?" Pausing at the door, she locked her gaze on him.

"I'm back," hollered Uncle Charlie from the rear of the store, tearing through the tension.

Knox darted his gaze from his uncle to Cate and then back again, sending him into a cloud of confusion at his uncle's drastic change in demeanor.

"Catie-bird," Charlie chirped, "See who's back in town? I'm having a little company for the time being." He closed the gap between them.

Uncle Charlie beamed. Cate's presence clearly had an effect on the older man.

"An extra set of hands is a welcomed gift." Cate grinned just as a large, noisy family entered the store, calling for assistance in one of the aisles.

"That's my cue." Knox held her gaze a little longer than necessary before excusing himself from the conversation, allowing his uncle and Cate to review the reservations. Giving in to temptation, he sneaked a peek a couple of times while helping the out-of-towners, reeled in by the sweet familiar rhythm of her voice.

Once Knox had the family squared away, he resumed his position at the counter and refocused on counting the till, moving at warp speed to beat his uncle to the recycling, the sight of him limping earlier etched in his mind.

"Catch you later, Knox."

At the mention of his name, he lifted his gaze in time to see Cate slip out the front door. He paused momentarily, mulling over the lost opportunity to say more.

Chapter Two

The parking lot was nearly full by the time Cate made it to The Shack, squeezing her car into a tight spot next to a souped-up jeep with two surfboards jammed in the back. She recognized Eliza's vehicle parked front and center of the restaurant.

The aroma of Southern fried cooking reminded Cate of just how famished she was. A few quick steps up weather-beaten stairs, she entered through a creaky screen door that swung shut behind her. The restaurant was nothing fancy, which made Cate like it even more. Ramshackle picnic tables sprawled about in no particular order. Worn benches lined the walls to accommodate the overflow.

Cate surveyed the restaurant, hoping to catch a glimpse of her teenage brother, Jackson, who logged time at The Shack when he wasn't swimming. His six-foot frame made him appear older than he was, his lanky body mimicking a young adult giraffe. His arm span and long legs won him the state championship in butterfly and backstroke, and he was training to become the next Michael Phelps, or so their parents said.

Sure enough, Jackson barreled out of the kitchen with a steaming tray of shrimp burgers as a special delivery to the table where Cate was headed. She bit her lip for fear the manager would scold her brother again for carrying orders from the kitchen instead of having the customers pick up their food from the window like they were supposed to. "Sorry I'm late." Weaving through the crowd, Cate slipped into a saved seat right next to Eliza with her green-eyed boyfriend, Will.

Eliza slid a sweet tea in Cate's direction. "I ordered you the usual. No potato bun, of course."

"Thanks." She settled in, dropping her handbag under the table.

"What took you so long?" Eliza swirled the straw around in her sweet tea.

"I ran into an old *friend,*" Cate twisted her lips.

Eliza tilted her head. "Is that what you're calling him these days?"

"You knew he was here?" Cate puckered her forehead.

"Nope, but by the expression on your face, I assume he has arrived." Eliza nibbled on a salty fry from the shareable basket at their table. "Knox was bound to make an appearance sooner or later with Charlie heading in for surgery. His uncle filled me in when I dropped off the late-arrival packages the other day. Knox might not have been your fairytale prince, but the guy has always been loyal to his family. You can't fault him for that."

"I guess his big city dreams have changed because he's back here on Gull Island…"

"Right where he belongs," finished Eliza. "City life isn't all it's cracked up to be."

Will leaned in. "You'll have to get used to Knox being around, especially since I invited him to join us for supper." He motioned toward the entrance with an expectant grin.

Cate peered over to find Knox standing there

dressed in typical southern beach attire: a worn crew-neck T-shirt and faded shorts.

He removed his sunglasses and hooked them on the front of his shirt.

The two locked gazes for a brief moment, and then Cate quickly spun. She wrestled with her emotions, while outwardly welcoming him to the group.

Eliza scooted closer to Will, leaving an open space.

The other friends at the table shifted, moving the food aside to create room.

Trying to remain calm, Cate inhaled, her chest tightening.

When Knox arrived at the table, he sat in the only available spot, next to his former girlfriend.

The friends at the table showered Knox with "hellos" and "good to see yous."

Cate made quick adjustments to smooth down her shirt and hair.

"Hey," he said calmly, his gaze lingering.

The intimate setting was far different from Bait & Switch, and heat rose in her cheeks and her heart pattered with Knox sitting so close. She prayed he couldn't see it. "Um, how's your uncle feeling, Knox?" Cate softly asked.

"A man of few words. I'm sure I'll learn more over the next few days," he said, in between stolen bites of Cate's fries.

Cate sipped her sweet tea. "Is that how long you'll be staying?"

"Depends," Knox replied.

The group exchanged light-hearted banter, getting reacquainted with Knox and catching up on the whereabouts of his extended family.

Jennifer Vido

Having finished her meal, Cate shifted in her seat, as a large party hovered close by eyeing their table of eight. Taking the hint, she nudged Eliza, motioning for the rest to follow suit.

"I'll collect the trash." Knox popped one last onion ring into his mouth. On his way to the trash receptacle in the corner, Knox hesitated when Will grabbed his arm and whispered something in his ear.

Cate leaned into Eliza. "What's up?"

Her friend shrugged.

Knox and Will joined the girls while the others said their goodbyes.

"If you don't mind, I'm going to catch a ride with Knox," Will said to Eliza. "It's been a while. Text you later?" He lightly brushed her cheek with his lips.

"Of course." Eliza squeezed his arm.

"I could use an extra set of hands anyway," Cate interjected. "I'm moving into Grammy's beach house for the summer."

Knox paused mid-step. "Really?"

Fishing her lanyard with keys attached out of her pocket, Cate nodded, pleased her subtle hint made him think twice.

Meanwhile Eliza and Will veered toward the exit.

Cate and Knox trailed behind.

"I must've missed something. Is Grammy ill?" Knox held open the screen door.

Cate passed by. She still got a tingly feeling whenever Knox displayed his proper Southern manners. "Nope. Healthy as a horse. Never been better."

"So, you're staying there because…"

"My family is living in Maine for the summer, leaving the house vacant. My brother and I are staying

18

there for a few months." She paused to catch her breath. "It'll cut down on my commute, and more importantly, I'll be able to keep an eye on Jackson." She relaxed her shoulders.

"Makes sense. The shorter commute, the greater chance of being on time, and some sibling bonding. I get it," reasoned Knox.

Cate crossed her arms, conceding her chronic tardiness was no secret, especially for her former boyfriend.

"So, I guess we will be seeing more of each other, especially if I stick around for a while," his voice lingered.

Lifting her chin, Cate focused on his deep blue eyes. "If I remember correctly, your preference is to wander, not put down roots." The blaring sound of Eliza's car horn cut short their conversation. "Sorry. I don't want to keep Eliza waiting. She's following me back to the cottage to help. Lots of boxes to unpack and sort through. Gotta go before she changes her mind." Impulsively, she leaned in for a friendly hug before heading straight to the car, giving no backward glance to gauge his reaction. Not even a wave goodbye.

****

Knox cut across the gravel parking lot, searching for his rented pickup truck, spotting Will in the front seat with his head down, likely messing around on his phone. He was relieved his friend didn't witness Cate hugging him. He'd hate for Will to read more into it. Yet for some reason, all he could think about right then was having her back in his arms. Being so close stirred up emotions he long ago put away. Closing his eyes, he breathed in the faint whiff of her perfume on his shirt.

Coming to his senses, he quickened his pace with gravel crunching underfoot to meet up with Will.

Knox left the truck unlocked and windows rolled down, not uncommon for someone from a small town. With a quick "hey, man," he climbed in and buckled up. He started the engine and shifted into gear, wise to where he was headed, the southernmost tip of Gull Island.

Years might have passed since Knox was on the island, but he traveled with ease on the winding roads. Per usual, the summer visitors mucked up traffic, which didn't bother him. He used the bonus time to catch up with Will; the conversation flowed naturally, as if no time had passed.

When seeing an old buck venturing into the road for handouts from curious vacationers, Knox perked up. "Theo!" The deer had a striking resemblance to one he named as a teenager.

"Remember how the Harvey twins teased you mercilessly about your so-called pet deer?"

"How could I forget the running joke in junior high?" Little did Knox's friends fully comprehend what solace the animal provided when he struggled with his relationship with his parents. "Theo and I had an understanding. With a little lettuce in hand, we became fast friends." To this day, his heart held a soft spot for the island's tame wildlife.

At the halfway point on Egret Way, the paved street turned into a dusty, dirt road. The homes at this end of the island blended into the natural habitat. "Take a peek at the eco-friendly architecture flanked by beach vegetation," said Knox. "The new homes replacing the old bungalows are being done right."

"The influx of visitors has sparked a surge in new construction," Will explained.

"I appreciate the effort to incorporate the native landscape into the structures," said Knox. "Living in the city didn't change me much. I'm still a naturalist at heart." He parked the truck on the side of the road along with a smattering of other vehicles. No designated parking places existed to utilize—just dirt, seagrass, and sand dunes. Depending on the tide, more spaces were available at certain times of day. The tall sea grass camouflaged the path to the beach. Locals knew by rote which way to go.

The friends strolled along a creaky boardwalk, taking in the sounds of nature, the tree frogs singing, and the crashing of waves on the shoreline. The sun slowly descended in the sky. Soon dusk would arrive.

"Even though I haven't been here in years, in some ways, Gull Island still feels like home. There's something about being in a small town, especially with family and friends," said Knox.

"This view never gets old." Will picked up a seashell and tucked it into his pocket.

At Will's side, he made his way toward a cluster of sandy rocks down by the shoreline. Knox noticed they weren't the only ones there. With the best view of the sunset on the island, locals and visitors alike flocked to the secluded area to relax, take selfies, and breathe in the salty air. He eyed a young couple, hand in hand, strolling by deep in conversation—a sight commonly seen in this particular area. His attention strayed toward the seagulls lazily floating on warm currents with the day winding down while beachcombers searched the tide line for shells and other hidden treasures.

"Let's head over there." Knox pointed. As luck would have it, they scored a prime spot. He heaved himself up on a blackish rock, covered in remnants from the sea with a dusting of sand.

Will copied his friend and mounted a similar one to his left.

"From what I can tell, Cate hasn't changed at all." His curiosity about her relationship status outweighed the risk of Will suspecting his interest.

"She's up for a promotion at Guest Services," Will said. "The manager is leaving to be with family in Atlanta, and Cate applied for the position. She'll probably get it, if she can show up on time for the interview."

"Does she still set all her clocks ahead five minutes?" Knox picked up a reed and drew circles on the rock's surface in the scattered sand.

"Eliza says so, but it doesn't seem to help her. It's hard to get ahead, when in reality, you're always behind." Will withdrew the seashell from his pocket and set it on his rock.

"I can't tell you how many times I've waited for her," he reminisced. "We're polar opposites when it comes to time management." Knox tossed the reed aside, replacing it with his phone. He snapped a pic of the sunset. "What's Eliza up to these days?"

"She's working at Guest Services as well, but just part-time. Her paintings have been featured in a couple of gallery exhibits in Charleston. She's trying to break into the art world with the goal of eventually being a full-time artist."

"I always believed she'd follow her passion. What's everyone else been up to?" Knox leaned in closer, allowing his friend to provide a rapid-fire update on his former classmates without disruption.

By the time Will had exhausted the list, the sun had set.

Knox glanced at his phone. "My uncle is expecting me back at Bait & Switch to help with closing. Time to go." He noticed stragglers passing by on their way back to the parking area. Soon the beach would be deserted, leaving only moonlight shining on the sand. Knox led the way to the truck. "Is Cate...um, seeing anyone?"

"Nah, she hasn't dated in months. I've set her up with a couple of my friends, but she's not interested. From what Eliza has told me, Cate's too busy trying to get her career off the ground."

"If she's interested in moving up the corporate ladder, she might want to think about finding a job in Charleston or Atlanta," Knox suggested.

"She'd rather make her mark here than take some sophisticated job far away."

Knox wondered if Will's comment was directed at him or if he was interpreting Cate's way of thinking. He didn't exactly leave the island on good terms.

"None of us want to leave," Will tucked his hands in his pockets. "Gull Island is our home. Yours, too."

Debating if he believed it to be true, Knox didn't reply. Inside the truck, he cranked the AC to cool the cabin. "How do you like working for your dad's company?" He steered back onto the main route.

"Business is booming on the island. Keeping up with the demand for new construction is challenging, but we like it that way. The company is focusing on building eco-friendly homes, which is far more complex than we've done in the past. If we want to stay relevant in the market, we need to get ahead of the trends, which involves risk. We could use an experienced photographer to showcase our work on the company website. Any clue where I'd find someone with a skilled eye behind the lens?" Will raised his eyebrows.

"Ah, man. I'm here to help my uncle." Knox caught a glimpse of him before narrowing his focus on the road. "I don't plan on staying more than a couple of weeks or so."

"You sure?"

"My career takes me all over the world," he insisted.

"And now you are here. Think about it. That's all I ask."

"Fair enough, but I'm not making any promises."

****

Bright and early the following day, Cate readied for a brisk jaunt on the beach dressed in her typical athletic shorts and a loose-fitting T-shirt. She tied her light-brown hair in a sloppy bun to beat the heat. Exhausted didn't even come close to describing her after yesterday's drama. Moving into the cottage was the first step toward her independence. Between Eliza grilling her for deets about her initial reaction to Knox to the menagerie of boxes and random items still needing to be sorted, she and her pounding head required fresh air.

While the more modern properties were located on Tidewater Beach at the southern end of the island near Bait & Switch, Grammy's beach cottage on Oceanview Drive was situated at the north end of the island. Here summer dwellings at various stages of renovations and expansions were passed to successive generations. Cate fancied how these hardy, original homes weathered the tropical storms throughout the years. Their rich character matched her determination to make living on the island a permanent thing.

This area boasted typical island features, like outside showers for rinsing off after a long day at the beach. Cate remembered fondly gazing up at the big, blue sky as spurts of water from the finicky spout washed over her sandy skin. The houses were raised with deep crawl spaces to allow for occasional high tides rising to their level.

During storms, Cate used to tease Grammy about jumping off the railing into a raft, an idea quickly put to rest. Carports were erected instead of garages, and usually the homes included two gravel parking spots for golf carts. Yellow accents on Grammy's cart matched the house. The other was plain white. Hardly anyone drove a car once on the island, unless an out-of-town visitor or someone just spending the day.

Cate's "new" summer dig, Grammy's clapboard cottage with its inviting buttercream yellow facade and white hurricane shutters, possessed spectacular oceanside views from every angle. Sliding glass doors revealed a row of white-painted rocking chairs beckoning from the screened-in porch. An assortment of used beach towels, most likely those of Jackson's friends Cate surmised, hung over the banister of the attached deck.

From the deck, Cate descended the stairs, breathing in the salty sea air. She glided her hand down the familiar banister worn smooth by years of sandy hands, with her suntanned face basking in the warmth of the sun. At the landing, rusty beach chairs and half-inflated floats rested against the barely used grill overtaken by weeds. A swarm of angry wasps hovered by ready to strike. Cate ducked to stay out of harm's way, making a mental note to call the exterminators upon her return. She had grand plans for those chairs and floats this summer.

Following the wooden planks, she traipsed through the tall seagrass to the sand. The sun made its way high in the sky as morning shrimp boats set sail for a full day of fishing. In the distance, she spotted Mayor Sam Heyward and his wife, Nell, riding bikes along the sandy lane, two constant figures in the neighboring community.

Ol' Man Henry, a retired schoolteacher and coach, dilly-dallied near the shoreline with his metal detector in search of lost treasures.

Cate waved an arm to catch his attention. A bellowed hello carried by the wind greeted her. Despite the years, some things never changed. The island remained a place for her to call home. She peeked at her phone. Achieving her fitness goal of ten thousand steps before starting her shift would require quickening her pace. If she wanted to get a big promotion, she needed to show initiative. In her mind, arriving on time, or even early for a change, would make an excellent first step.

Around the bend, Cate did a double-take when she sighted a vacant lot that used to hold a three-story house. The former home belonged to a prominent island family. Curious, Cate veered toward its direction. Making her way through the seagrasses and prickly vegetation, she encountered two black-haired men, one rather tall and the other medium build. As she got closer, she cracked a smile. "Will? Is that you?" She trudged through the white, powdery sand, her feet sinking with every step.

The two men pivoted and squinted in her direction, the hot sun obstructing their view. Will was holding what appeared to be blueprints, while his dad carried a clipboard with a legal pad affixed.

"Hey, Cate," Will shouted.

Mr. Purdey waved her over.

Bypassing a sand dune, she quickened her step. "What are you doing out here so early on a Sunday morning?"

"When you operate your own business, every day is a working day, especially during our busiest season," Mr. Purdey explained.

"Surprised to see you up so early," Will said.

Cate laughed. "I couldn't sleep last night. Figured I might as well get up and exercise before I head to work. Guest Services is a zoo on Sundays. Lots of people coming and going."

"Will told me you're up for a big promotion, Catie-bird." The older man crossed his arms over his broad chest.

"News travels fast." She gave Will the stink eye for his loose lips. "What happened to the Hugers' house? All that's left is this wide-open space." She directed her comments to Will's dad.

"To get you up to speed on the project, the house suffered from a structural defect. Only option was to tear it down and start from scratch." Will took the lead, opening the blueprints and pointing out the new structural design. "Right here, these are the eco-friendly features."

With Will's eye for design and his father's business acumen, Cate suspected things were taking off for this family-run enterprise.

"My dad's propensity for naturalistic building elements is key to our signature style."

She had an overwhelming sense of awe and admiration, realizing her friend's forward-thinking green designs would lead to exponential growth on the island and beyond.

Mr. Purdey excused himself to take a phone call from a subcontractor.

While he dealt with business, Cate and Will explored the lot, taking in the magnificent views of the ocean.

Soaking up every detail Will shared, Cate asked questions about the design and how each detail would fit into the master plan. "No secret. The Huger family was one of the first settlers on the island. Redesigning their summer home will certainly be a game-changer."

"No doubt, a big contract for our growing firm. As a matter of fact, I mentioned to Knox last night that we could use his talents to promote this project. Before and after pictures on the website and social media would put Purdey & Son on the larger map. Think you could convince him?"

Cate shook her head. "I doubt Knox will listen to me. He tends to have a mind of his own. As soon as Uncle Charlie is on the mend, he'll be back on the road to his next exotic location. Sorry to be the bearer of bad news, even if it is the truth. Knox never stays put in one place too long and that includes Gull Island."

"Perhaps with someone like you in his life, he

would reconsider." He stared her squarely in the eye.

"Not likely. His wanderlust needs to be fed." Cate scoffed.

"Maybe he's come back to Gull Island to set down roots." Will shrugged.

Cate planted her hands on her hips. "I gave up on Knox a long time ago. You should, too." She refused to entertain the idea of Knox being a part of their lives, not when he broke her heart and disappointed others. She circumvented the lot, stomping her way back to Mr. Purdey.

Will's father still talked on his phone, pacing back and forth near the sea grasses gently bending in the breeze. Mr. Purdey disconnected his call. "Sun is shining, missy. If you don't get on your way, the guests will be lining up at your door."

"Yes, time for me to go," she said, thankful for the timely reminder. "Nice to see you again, Mr. Purdey." She leaned close to Will. "We'll talk later." No need for her to say much more. She was still flushed with mixed emotions from the impromptu sightings of Knox the day prior.

Heading toward the boardwalk, she understood that being so close to Knox tested her willpower. Falling for him—his broad shoulders, his sexy smile, his charm, and charisma—a second time would be too easy. Hurt once by him, Cate had no intention of letting it happen again.

Chapter Three

The warmth of the morning sun awakened Knox from a deep sleep. He hadn't understood how tired he was until his head hit the pillow late last night. Being back in his old room in Uncle Charlie's house evoked many memories. Some were good, and others were not so good. The familiar smell of black pepper bacon frying eased Knox out of bed. He grabbed a ratty T-shirt and a well-loved pair of gray sweatpants from his duffle bag to throw on, not wanting to rock the boat by showing up underdressed at his uncle's table.

Heading downstairs, he heard the cracking sound of fresh farm eggs and steered toward the kitchen. For as long as Knox could remember, his uncle sourced most of his food from local farmers near Beaufort. The freshness of the ingredients made up for his uncle's lack of cooking skills. The limited menu at Bait & Switch directly reflected this fact. Although, if food was rated by the amount of heart put into its preparation, certainly his uncle would achieve five stars.

"'Bout time you got out of bed." His uncle barked orders similar to those of an army cook.

Knox set the table, poured the coffee, and plated breakfast in no time. Carrying the ketchup and hot sauce in the crook of an arm, he swiped the pitcher of orange juice off the countertop with his free hand and sat in his chair. He poured two tall glasses before he and his uncle tucked into their meal.

Despite the disapproving grimace from Uncle Charlie, Knox doused the scrambled eggs on his plate in hot sauce. He slathered a generous pat of butter on the burnt toast in an attempt to choke down the charred edges. Doctoring up food made it palatable most days, and today was no exception.

"Cate drops by the store every day after five. Think you can get used to that, or am I going to find you hiding behind the counter whenever she comes in? Just wanted to prepare ahead of time. I don't like surprises." His uncle slurped his coffee.

Knox choked on a piece of bacon.

His uncle patted him on the back. "I'll take that as you'll be hiding on the floor. Word travels fast in this town."

When they finished eating, Knox took charge, clearing the dishes and loading them in the dishwasher. He noticed his uncle hobbling toward the bathroom. "Are we going to talk about it?"

His uncle paused in the doorway, shoulders slumped. "I'm having a hip replacement. Plain and simple. I'll be in the hospital for a few days. Recovery time is four to six weeks, give or take."

Knox swallowed hard, his gaze fixated on the back of his uncle's head, making it easy to invent a plausible excuse on the fly. Four to six weeks was a long time to stay in one place, especially with Cate being near. He assumed the stay would be a week, two at the most. Four to six never crossed his mind.

No wonder his father was vague with the details. Nevertheless, here he was, standing in his uncle's kitchen, with a man who meant the world to him. How could he shirk his responsibilities? The only person he could trust with the job was himself. "I'll stay," he replied with conviction.

"Get showered, young man. We have chores to do."

Knox listened to his uncle's voice falter, throat constricting as his eyes watered. He did as he was told. Having to put his career on hold would set him back professionally. Still, focusing on his uncle's care forced any doubt out of his mind that he was doing the right thing.

****

Cate returned to the beach cottage at eight o'clock. Her shift started in an hour. Not much time to get showered and out the door, but she was determined to make it work. Wandering down the hall past her bedroom, she cringed at the sight of the mountain of clothes on the floor, begging to be organized and put away in her antique bureau and closet. Maybe tomorrow. In Grammy's sizable bedroom, she ran her fingertips along the heirloom bedpost, making a mental note to remind Jackson to gather up Grammy's chairs to take to the repair shop in Beaufort.

Ten minutes later, she inspected her freshly showered self in the mirror, uniform polo and khaki shorts intact.

"Did you leave me any hot water?" Jackson's muffled voice called from his room, likely buried under the covers.

"The only way to find out is to get out of bed and see." She popped her head in the doorway and flipped on the light.

The sound of the cuckoo clock ticking loudly in the kitchen nudged her toward the door. With no time to pack a lunch, she rummaged in the refrigerator and scored a snack-size, nonfat, vanilla Greek yogurt and a shiny red apple. She tucked a slim can of chilled peach seltzer in her favorite quilted crossbody bag and shuffled out the back door.

Eyeing her phone in the front seat of the golf cart, Cate calculated an extra fifteen minutes of leeway. Plenty of time for a quick stop at The Wise Owl for the daily special, vanilla iced cappuccino. She could use the extra jolt of caffeine to get her through the typical busy Sunday shift.

The circle, the area of shops commonly referred to by locals, was jammed with early beachgoers with the same idea. The line at the coffee shop snaked out the door, not a good sign if she wanted to arrive at work on time. Peering ahead, she spotted a familiar head of sandy-blond hair. She chewed her lip for a moment, then politely excused herself as she negotiated her way through the line.

Drawing a deep breath, Cate mustered her courage. "There you are, Knox. Sorry I'm late." She flashed a pageant smile to a mature couple standing between her and a cup of cold brew.

The young man with broad shoulders pivoted. When he and Cate locked gazes, a smile crossed his lips. "No problem. I saved you a spot."

The pair obliged.

Cate leaned in close. "I owe you one."

"I'd say you do. I've been standing patiently in a line that has been moving at a snail's pace. To what do I owe the pleasure?"

"I'm on my way to work"—she pointed to the building visible from where they stood—"and figured it would be a good idea to fuel up before I faced the visitors. Popular day for signing up for excursions and activities."

Despite having plenty of space, Knox inched closer with every word she uttered.

Not that she was complaining, mind you. His earthy scent instantly evoked a familiarity she realized she had missed. His lips, with a hint of a smile, still softened her heart.

"Cate?"

His voice interrupted her musings. Such a long time had passed since she daydreamed about Knox, especially in that way. His being temporarily on Gull Island stirred feelings she put to rest. The sole purpose for her living here for the summer was to get a new lease on life by landing the big promotion at Guest Services. Getting involved with someone from her past was not part of the plan, especially someone who broke her heart. Quickly, she rebounded. "How's Uncle Charlie?"

Before he could respond, they advanced in line and entered the building. Like most places on the island, space was limited with the counter taking up the majority of the room along with a handful of tables and stools.

"He's having a hip replacement," he said matter-of-factly. "Six weeks of recuperation time."

Cate swallowed hard, fearing the answer to the question that warranted being asked. "Will you be able to stay?"

"May I help you?" the teenage girl behind the

counter asked.

Knox ordered. "Two iced cappuccinos, please." He withdrew ten dollars from his wallet and handed it to the cashier. "My treat," he whispered in Cate's ear.

His boyish grin warmed Cate's heart, like two fifteen-year-olds in love. "Thank you for the morning pick-me-up." She moved to the prep area for cold drinks.

"To answer your question, yes. I plan on sticking around as long as my uncle needs me. Not sure what I'll do about the gigs I have already booked. I'm guessing they'll need to be postponed, or maybe the company can hire another freelancer. Not my problem. My energy will be focused on my uncle's care. The rest will eventually fall into place." He sipped his iced cold brew through a paper straw.

An idea popped into Cate's head, planted by Will earlier. "In the meantime, why don't you help Will's dad with the promotional material for their business? Use that marketing experience you got up north. It'll give you something else to focus on in the downtime. Your uncle is going to require plenty of rest to heal properly. Only so much you can do for him."

"But, I'll need to take my uncle to therapy," he replied.

"No worries." Cate waved her hands. "A couple of the fishermen volunteered to pitch in."

"Oh…good. That's nice of them. Um, it'll give me more time for meal prep." He shifted back on his heels.

"Meals are covered. Ol' Man Henry made a sign-up sheet. Traipsed all over town to get every slot filled. Your uncle is a popular guy around here."

He stepped closer and rested his hand on her

shoulder. "Almost nine o'clock. What time does your morning shift begin?"

Cate shoved the half-empty cappuccino in his free hand. "This conversation isn't over. Thanks for the coffee. Next one's on me. Off to Bait & Switch to pick up the reservation book and leftover welcome packages." A clever way of covering up that she was running late…again.

****

Knox opted for the long route to Bait & Switch to mull over the seed Will and Cate planted about temporarily working for Purdey & Son. Granted, he'd be in the area for an extended period, but his main priority would be his uncle, not some side hustle. Without experience as a caregiver, he'd have his work cut out for him. Once Uncle Charlie's mobility improved, Knox figured the challenge would be to keep his uncle out of harm's way. Coming up with creative ideas to make his uncle's rehab feel less restrictive would be no easy task. A body's rate of healing was no match for a capable mind and a man used to doing things his own way. The potential for a fall would be a setback neither of them could afford. The sooner Uncle Charlie healed, the sooner Knox could leave Gull Island and return to his own life.

The store was another responsibility. Bait & Switch was like a well-oiled machine. His uncle hired plenty of seasonal help in the summer months, which would come in handy during his hiatus. Knox believed finding a grill cook to replace his uncle wouldn't be an issue; in fact, he was pretty sure one of the summer staff could handle the job. Heck, business might even pick up with someone else manning the spatula. Thank goodness the tourists kept the store afloat with impulse grocery items and souvenir shopping. Knox planned on working the front counter, keeping tabs on the cash flow…and Cate.

Bumping into her at The Wise Owl awakened feelings Knox put to bed years ago. His focus needed to be on caring for the one person in his life who never let him down. Yet, his mind was consumed with Cate—her laugh, her smile, her inability to make it anywhere on time. She hadn't changed one bit. Being in close proximity would be a challenge. He hoped his present circumstances, well-intentioned as they were, would not end up creating more problems.

Although his dawdling killed a little time, if he didn't get to the shop soon, his uncle would be grilling him on his whereabouts. Getting from the house to Bait & Switch didn't take long. No use in trying to avoid the truth. If he admitted to grabbing a coffee with Cate, maybe his uncle would let it be. No use stirring up trouble where none existed.

Right inside the back door of the store, Knox could hear Cate's voice, bubbly with laughter. Stuffing his keys in his front pocket, he headed toward the noise.

"Like I said to my nephew, I don't expect to be recuperating the full six weeks. I viewed some online instructional videos about the surgery. I plan on being back on my feet in no time."

"And I will be monitoring his every step to ensure he doesn't overdo it," Knox called out. When he neared them, he couldn't help but notice the grin on Cate's face. Encouraged by her warmth, he continued, "Good morning. Nice to see you."

"Picking up the leftover visitor packages on my

way into work." She angled her head and winked.

"Good idea to stop here first." Knox gave a slight nod. He noticed the twinkle in Uncle Charlie's eye. He, too, appeared to be smitten with Cate and well aware of her tendency to race against the clock in the morning.

"I'll let you two catch up," Charlie said. "In the meantime, I'll grab the reservation book upstairs. Last I checked, we received at least fifteen requests for either dolphin excursions or alligator tours. Not as many for fishing trips or kayaking tours."

"I see a good, old-fashioned notebook is still used to keep track of the after-hours bookings, most likely due to my uncle's reluctance to embrace modern technology." Knox handed it to Cate.

"If it ain't broke, why fix it?" Charlie shouted from the staircase.

As soon as he was out of earshot, Cate came clean. "Today's my big interview. I couldn't risk being late."

He leaned in closer. "Just be you. You're the right person for the job, or so Will reports."

"Listen, Knox, I'm aware our conversation was interrupted earlier, but seriously won't you please consider helping out Will's family business? I was talking to him this morning on my walk, and I know they are actively seeking help with marketing strategies, in addition to photographs of their new developments. Someone talented like you with razor-sharp marketing skills and professional photography experience could put a company like Purdey & Son on the map. Probably be easy stuff compared to what you're used to. Think about it. You'd be helping an old friend while making a difference here on Gull Island."

Knox heaved a sigh. "My main objective is to help

my uncle get better, not start a new job in South Carolina. I'm flattered by your vote of confidence, but I've already committed to a few freelance gigs once I leave here. I think I'll stick to the original plan. Keep things simple."

Uncle Charlie lingered not far behind them, talking with a customer. After finishing with his conversation, he shifted closer and handed Cate the reservation book. "Here you go, Catie-bird. Thanks for stopping by."

"See you later," she replied in her signature sing-song voice, and off she marched.

The door barely closed before Uncle Charlie inserted his unsolicited opinion. "Purdey & Son is a reputable firm. Eco-friendly and professional. Idle hands are the tools of the devil, young man. You might want to think about the offer."

Knox was not the least bit surprised. Uncle Charlie meddled in his business without a hint of hesitation. Like the time Knox decided to throw in the towel with surfboarding. Try as he might, he couldn't catch a wave. The following day, his uncle dragged him back to the surf and took it upon himself to teach him the basics. To this day, Knox credited his uncle for his slightly above-average surfing skills.

The usual morning bustle kept Knox and Uncle Charlie busy, leaving little time for further discussion. People with familiar faces stopped by, welcoming Knox back to town. Even Ol' Man Henry made a point of saying hello, reminiscing about Knox's winning home run in the state championship game. Knox spent more time talking than actually working.

By noon, the constant stream of customers thinned. Knox rounded up two summer helpers to staff the front counter, enabling him to grill a couple of juicy cheeseburgers for his uncle and himself. His grumbly stomach begged to be filled. Knox grabbed a large bag of salty chips and two bottles of icy cold cola and went to the backroom with his uncle one step ahead.

An old recliner salvaged from a vacant rental property occupied much of the room, leaving barely enough space for a card table, two worn folding chairs, and a twin-size cot. Faded posters and old flyers dressed up the cream-colored walls. A tiny window with a torn shade let in natural sunlight.

Each assumed his designated spot, Uncle Charlie near the window and Knox by the door. The two wasted no time and got busy eating their mouth-watering burgers and crunchy chips. Wiping his mouth with a crumpled paper towel, Knox initiated the conversation. "I rushed back to help you, not work for someone else. If I invest time in Purdey & Son, people will come to expect more than I can give. You understand, don't you?"

"Able or willing? A big difference, son." Uncle Charlie folded his hands.

The words stung. "Not that simple. I let people down before and already live with past guilt. I'd be setting myself up for failure."

"Cate and Will are willing to give you a second chance. Why not have a little faith in yourself and see how it goes? You're already here." His uncle rooted through the bag for remnants, popping bits of crinkle-cut chips into his mouth.

"Let's focus on your surgery. Deal?" Knox stalled.

"For now," Uncle Charlie acquiesced.

A rap on the door signaled their need to get back to

work. Knox wiped off the crumbs on the table with a spare napkin while gathering the trash. Helping his uncle to his feet, he squeezed his shoulder.

A young couple joined Knox at the front counter, occupying his full attention.

"We're debating between a dolphin tour and a sunset boat ride," explained the smitten boyfriend. "Care to weigh in?"

"Just depends on what you're in the mood for. If you want an adventure, go for the dolphin tour. Plenty of them to see this time of year. If you're in luck, you might even come across a manatee. The sunset boat ride is more of a relaxing, sightseeing cruise around the island. Either way you can't go wrong," he advised.

"You pick," said the guy.

"Let's go with the dolphin tour." She wrapped her arms around her partner's waist and snuggled in tight.

"You've made a good choice," Knox replied. "I'll take care of that reservation."

Their light-hearted banter reminded him of how he and Cate used to be. One wanted one thing, and the other wanted something else. If only they'd agreed to meet each other halfway. Maybe things would have been different.

Thinking back to his last romantic sunset cruise with Cate triggered feelings of shame about what happened afterward. Picturing her face in his rearview mirror as he drove away would forever be ingrained in his mind. At the time, he believed leaving her behind was the best solution. Their goals were not aligned. He wanted to experience life outside of South Carolina, whereas Cate never intended to leave her family or friends. He blindsided her by avoiding a serious conversation about their future. Years later, he still couldn't get her off his mind.

Knox distractedly wiped down the counter with lemon-scented cleaner, weighing the pros and cons of freelancing at Purdey & Son. A pragmatist at heart, he focused on the positives rather than the negatives. If something else could occupy his free time, Knox would be foolish not to take advantage of it.

The first step involved having a plan in place to avoid over-committing himself. One project at a time would be the best strategy. Social media platforms were his specialty, both for businesses and celebrity types. Ironically, his social life was nowhere to be found on the web. Quite simply, he refused to post anything about his personal life. Yet, in hindsight, maybe if he embraced it, he'd be privy to the current goings-on in Cate's life. The mere thought of it gave him pause.

Glancing at his watch, he realized her interview should be well over by now. He wondered if she dazzled her boss with her go-getter attitude and warm smile. Who was he kidding? Cate was probably on the office's desktop, selecting a personalized nameplate for her new office door.

Chapter Four

"Good morning. I've already grabbed the reservation book and packets from Bait & Switch." Cate breezed in the front door to Guest Services. The line of people waiting to check in was longer than usual at the start of the day.

Behind the counter, Eliza cradled the cordless phone between her neck and shoulder while entering information on the laptop stationed at the counter.

Answering calls while working the desk was par for the course for a small operation like Gull Island Guest Services. The guests greatly outnumbered the employees. Immediately, Cate made eye contact with her. Eliza's quick nod toward the office affirmed the boss had already arrived. Skirting the cozy beige couches and a wooden coffee table laden with local seashells artfully displayed, Cate slipped behind the desk to pitch in, stowing the reservation book in its proper place and setting the welcome packets on the counter. Quickly hiding her belongings in the bottom drawer for the time being, she waved the next guest over to get the line moving.

Cate's boss, Kelsey Durbin, emerged from her office. Heading toward the front door, the stylish brunette chatted with those waiting in line to ease their frustration with the unexpected wait time. Small paper cups filled with freshly made lemonade were distributed to quench the guests' thirst. Tempting trays of sweet, bite-sized pastries near the front desk offered the Southern genteel culture of both satiating hunger's edge and keeping interactions pleasant while waiting in line. A true Lowcountry welcome for out-of-town arrivals.

Working in tandem, Cate and Eliza focused solely on their clients. They handed out welcome packages to the Sunday arrivals, booked excursions, and answered the same questions repeatedly with friendly smiles.

When the phone rang, Cate took charge by answering the calls. Whether it be doling out recommendations or putting out fires with hard-to-please guests, she was on it. Peering in Kelsey's direction, she met her boss's slight nod of praise. The timing couldn't be better for Cate to shine.

"Please join me in my office, Cate. I'd like to discuss the open position and what it entails," Kelsey said at the first sign of a lull in the action.

Behind the counter, Cate discreetly squeezed Eliza's hand.

"Good luck," Eliza whispered.

Cate treaded purposefully, taking her time, so as to not appear anxious or nervous about the interview.

"Eliza, please hold my calls." Kelsey didn't wait for a response. She simply ushered Cate into her office and closed the glass door to give them some privacy.

Cate steadied her gaze, observing Kelsey amble over to the opposite side of the glossy, white-lacquered desk and sit in her office chair. A petite fortysomething woman, she wore a navy sheath dress with gold accents paired with wedge heels. Cate admired Kelsey's medium-sized hoop earrings that completed her signature style.

Despite her trembling knees, Cate waited until her boss invited her to sit down. She intended to follow business protocol to the letter to show how well-suited she was for the job.

"Please be seated." Kelsey motioned toward the vacant chair.

"Yes, ma'am." Cate eased into the seat.

"Busy Sunday morning," Kelsey commented. Glancing at a sheet of paper on her desk, she picked up a yellow pencil and scribbled a note before giving Cate her full attention.

"Gull Island is *the* summer destination here in the Lowcountry. We have miles of sandy beaches, sports and leisure activities, and the most picturesque sunsets on the East Coast," Cate spewed without taking a breath.

Kelsey raised a brow. "Spoken like a true resort professional. Gull Island has all that and more. And who better than a qualified Guest Services manager to introduce this beautiful island to its visitors."

Cate's heart pounded in her chest. Her dream job was literally at her fingertips. A door of opportunity was waiting to be opened. Now was the time to step on through.

"I'm sad to be leaving," Kelsey continued, "but family obligations are calling me back to Atlanta. Timing isn't the best with it being smack dab in the middle of the summer season." Kelsey leafed through a stack of papers. "I've received close to twenty-five qualified applicants to fill the position from various resort towns on the Eastern seaboard."

"I'm willing to learn whatever you think I need to

take this position and run with it," Cate replied with her shoulders back and head held high. "I might not be the most qualified on paper, but I most certainly have the day-to-day experience needed to successfully meet the needs of Gull Island's guests." Cate drew in a breath in anticipation of Kelsey's reply.

"I couldn't agree more." Kelsey folded her hands.

"You do?" Cate blurted.

"You've come a long way since we first met. I've seen your growth and dedication to your job. The position is yours on one condition." Kelsey narrowed her gaze.

"Name it." Cate scooted to the edge of her chair.

"You purchase an alarm clock." A mischievous grin slowly emerged from the corners of Kelsey's mouth. She carefully stood and gracefully skirted her desk to congratulate Cate with a brisk, firm handshake.

Cate followed her lead and clasped Kelsey's hand, suppressing her excitement to appear professional. When Kelsey's cell phone rang, Cate excused herself, grabbing hold of the doorknob and slipping out of the office to afford her boss some privacy. Bursting with pride, she locked gazes with Eliza from across the room, slightly nodding.

Between guests, she wasted no time sharing the big news via text with her circle of close friends. Knox did cross her mind, much to her surprise, but she'd have to wait to tell him in person. Deleting his number years ago seemed like a good idea at the time. She contemplated calling over to Bait & Switch at her next break but changed her mind. She didn't want to give him the wrong idea. His intentions were crystal clear. He was not sticking around. Luckily, Kelsey opted to leave early after sending rejection emails to other candidates, giving Cate and Eliza time for one last informal "boss away, time to play."

"First order of business, out with the cool neutral hues. I have paint swatches with shades of yellow stuffed in my bag. I grabbed them from the hardware store the other day. Want to see the colors?" Cate's enthusiasm bubbled over.

"See what I have?" Eliza held two bottles of cola. "Time to make some changes."

Cate's heart fluttered with hope for her future.

****

A typical Sunday night for Cate and Eliza entailed a stop at the pavilion, a popular hangout where they could hear the local musicians jam and catch up with friends. As summer was heating up, residents and visitors had a chance to wind down in the shade while sipping ice-cold beverages or supping on treats and such from the local food trucks. Music generally started at five o'clock, enabling those punching out for the day to join in the fun.

Guest Services closed right on time. Cate hopped in her golf cart parked out front and picked up Eliza toting a picnic blanket from the rear of the building. First stop was Bait & Switch to drop off the late-arrival packets and reservation book, and then drive to the pavilion shortly thereafter.

"While you were in Kelsey's office getting your big promotion, my mom called." Eliza held on to the overhead grab bar as the cart weaved in and out of traffic. "She and Dad snagged a last-minute dinner reservation with friends at their favorite restaurant on the waterfront in Beaufort. An impromptu get-together.

You don't mind staying in, do you? Sunday night is not the best day of the week to go out and celebrate your promotion."

Cate hesitated slightly. "Um, sure?" Pausing at the roundabout, she glimpsed at Eliza, trying to figure out what she was up to.

"And, you're probably wondering *why* we need to stay put," Eliza explained.

Her heart skipped a beat. Eliza was definitely up to something. A best friend wouldn't let an important occasion pass by without marking it with some sort of a celebration, Sunday night or not. "Go on." Cate eased off the gas pedal to take it all in.

"My parents adopted the most adorable Jack Russell terrier mix from Pretty Paws Rescue this morning. His name is Fripp, and he's only ten weeks old. I can't wait to meet him. Puppy kisses and puppy breath. What more could you want?"

Swerving to the right, Cate carefully avoided the unexpected pothole in the road, the irony not lost on her. "How can I say no to a puppy?"

Eliza clapped her hands. "Perfect. Mom picked up chicken salad, heirloom tomatoes, and freshly picked corn on the cob at the market today, all your favorites. Perfect ending to a long day."

"Sounds delicious," Cate acquiesced. "Let's take the shortcut to avoid getting stuck in traffic. You never know who we might bump into once we get there."

"Mm, hmm," Eliza murmured.

At the drop-off, Cate searched for Knox, who she found stuck at the counter with customers, three deep, making it impossible to catch him alone to share her big news.

****

When she arrived at the pavilion, Cate parked in her usual spot near the side entrance. "Will's already here." She pointed in his direction. The three friends made it a habit to meet here regularly, schedules permitting. "Grab him. Let's make our way over to the grass in front of the stage. Our usual spot is filling up fast."

"Congratulations, Ms. Newly Appointed Guest Services Manager," Will shouted.

Cate slowed her pace to allow Eliza a chance to greet her boyfriend first with a peck on the cheek before grabbing his attention. Cate gave him the abbreviated version of what happened, careful not to monopolize the conversation too much. The concert was on the verge of starting.

She made every effort to concentrate on the entertainment, but the excitement about her new job vied for her attention. As a manager, she'd have job security, benefits, and a clear career path within the company. Things were happening. The organizer in her was already making mental lists for the office, a must if she intended to hit the ground running.

Between acts, Cate excused herself, feeling the need to stretch her legs, while surveying the crowd for a certain someone with sandy-blond hair. Try as she might, she struck out and weaved her way back to Eliza and Will. Cate feigned interest as the couple swapped stories with a few high school friends. When the second band ended its set, Cate gathered her things, disappointed Knox hadn't surfaced.

The circle of friends followed her lead, making plans to meet again the following Sunday.

"Have you shared your big news with Knox?" Will shook out the crumbs from the blue checked blanket.

Cate wrinkled her nose. "Nah, he'll hear about it through the grapevine soon enough. He probably doesn't care anyway."

"Why do you say that?" He tucked it under his arm.

"He's only here to take care of his uncle. Not help you with your family business or stick his nose in mine. He's made it patently clear. Honestly, *nothing* is going on between the two of us." Her voice emphasized *nothing* more emphatically than she hoped, causing Will and Eliza to lock gazes. She was too tired to protest their disbelief. Instead, Cate forced a smile, signaling the topic was off-limits. Luckily, they picked up on her cue and dropped it for the time being. If all progressed as she expected, Knox would be packing his bags and heading for parts unknown.

On the way to the parking lot, several acquaintances rushed over to hug Cate and congratulate her on the new position. Despite her best attempt, an unexpected pinch of disappointment overshadowed her excitement. Cate ached to share her news with Knox.

"Cate, are you listening?"

"Yes, I mean. No. Sorry, Eliza. Please repeat what you just said," she replied.

"Let's go. Mom's expecting us back at the house pronto." She snapped her fingers.

"What happened to Will? He was just here." Cate searched the crowd.

Eliza paused a moment. "He…he had to leave." She checked her phone. "If we don't hurry, you'll miss seeing my parents. They're interested in hearing all about your big promotion. C'mon. Lead the way."

The co-workers recapped their work day as they headed toward the marsh located on the peninsula, not far from the parkland reserve. Cate focused on the positives, relegating Knox to the back of her mind. Her crowning achievement deserved a moment of glory with her loyal and supportive friend.

On Fiddlers Trace Drive, a line of golf carts cluttered the road. Not unusual on this particular street, as its magnificent view drew visitors and residents. Along the banks of the coastal salt marsh, the tall spartina grass grew prolifically, creating a natural habitat for wildlife. During low tide, the mud flats were home to an army of fiddler crabs.

"Remember how we used to try to catch those speedy little crabs?" Eliza double-tapped Cate's knee as she rolled into her parents' driveway.

"Surprise!" shouted a chorus of voices in the distance.

Cate jerked her head in the opposite direction, greeted by a bevy of friends streaming out the home's front door. She leaned over and hugged Eliza, appreciative of her hand in all of this. She smiled broadly and hop-skipped off the cart.

A tiny puppy emerged from a sea of legs and scampered down the front porch steps right onto Cate's lap. "This must be Fripp," she exclaimed amid sloppy puppy kisses. The light-brown-and-white bundle of energy tugged on Cate's long hair.

Eliza was quick to curtail the puppy's overzealous affection by luring it away with a tennis ball from the yard.

Cate embraced her well-wishers, squeezing hands

and kissing cheeks.

"Congrats, sis," shouted Jackson from the porch steps.

She waved hello to her little brother. Standing next to him was the one person she wanted to see, Knox. The two locked gazes for a brief moment.

Eliza's dad stuck his head out the front door. "Dinner is served."

The smell of homemade food wafted in the summer air, drawing Cate and the group into the air-conditioned house. Even the puppy ambled up the stairs in search of a bone or perhaps table scraps to chew. Despite it being the end of the day, the oppressive heat dictated eating indoors.

Cate opened her eyes wide at the sight of aluminum trays atop burners holding barbecued ribs, pulled pork, and creamy mac & cheese. Desserts consisting of summer berry pie, pound cake, and an assortment of homemade cookies occupied the center island. On the back deck, guests helped themselves to pitchers of sweet and unsweetened tea and coolers filled with water, cokes, and lemonade. Hungry from a long day's work, the friends fixed themselves a plate of cookout staples.

On the screened-in porch, country music sounded in the background while Cate visited with two friends who peppered her with questions about the new position.

Midway through their conversation, Jackson and Knox appeared in the doorway with plates piled high with home cooking.

The friends excused themselves to grab a plate.

"Did you leave any food for the rest of us?" Cate

teased.

Balancing a plate piled high with a barbeque sandwich and a generous helping of coleslaw, Knox used his free hand to retrieve a napkin and utensils tucked inside his front pant pocket. "Ran out of fingers," he explained with a twinkle in his eye.

Cate's infectious laugh filled the room.

Jackson set down his plate. "I'm heading back to the kitchen to grab two cold glasses of sweet tea. Need anything?"

Cate shook her head no.

"I hear congrats are in order." Knox cozied up on the couch. "You deserve it. You've poured your life into this job."

His sincerity tugged at her heart.

"Let me guess. First order of business will be a total Guest Services makeover. Am I right?" He bit into a freshly baked bun loaded with pork, slaw, and barbeque sauce.

Jackson handed Knox a glass of tea before joining them on the couch.

"Nailed it. Eliza and I brainstormed possible design options all afternoon. We even checked online for inexpensive office furniture. Depending on the budget, we'll see how much we get to do. First on my list will be to paint my new office…"

"Yellow." He wiped a drizzle of sauce from his chin with a crumpled napkin.

"That's right. Lemon-colored walls with navy-and-yellow-patterned drapes. A burst of sunshine to greet me each day." Her high-pitched voice mimicked her enthusiasm.

"Your office will match your personality. I like it

already."

Questions arose about her start date and the need to hire Cate's replacement. Filling her former position would be her first task as manager.

"If you're serious about taking me to the invitational swim meet, I'll ask my boss for the time off," Jackson butted in. "The sooner I do it, the better. He'll probably ask me to pick up extra shifts once I get back, but I'll manage. If I plan on swimming in college, I need to improve my times."

"Go ahead. I'm down. I never met a swim meet I didn't like," Knox kidded.

Cate perked up. "Knox, how did you find out about the swim meet?" If Knox was truly staying only until his uncle no longer needed him, how would he make good on a promise to her brother? Knox inched his head left and right, with a pointed stare at Jackson.

"Sounds like you two have it all figured out," Cate remarked, her words at odds with her unsettled emotions.

"We were catching up at the pavilion, and Jackson mentioned wanting to compete. I figured your new position would come with long hours, so I volunteered to step in if needed," Knox explained.

"Hmm...you're full of surprises." She raised an eyebrow, trying to figure out his game plan.

"Uncle Charlie will need a break from me at some point," Knox continued. "The preliminaries are on Saturday, the busiest day at Guest Services if memory serves me right. A win-win for all, as I see it."

Personable, reliable, and now involving himself in her family life. For someone so transitory, he appeared anything but. "Let me think about it," Cate swished around the ice in her cup.

"Of course." Knox grinned.

"Speaking of your uncle, what time do you need to be at the hospital tomorrow?" Cate uncrossed her legs, leaning in closer.

"Bright and early," Knox replied. "The surgery is scheduled for nine o'clock, with an eight arrival time. The plan is to hit the road by seven at the latest. Uncle Charlie is never late to anything, especially something as important as this. He's insisting on driving to Beaufort, one more spin behind the wheel before he's out of commission. We'll have to see about that."

Jackson eased off the couch, his phone vibrating in his back pocket. "It's for you." He put it on speaker and held it out.

"Congratulations, a well-earned promotion," gushed Grammy, amid happy tears. "I can't wait to get hold of one of your new business cards."

"You'll be the first," Cate assured her.

"Don't forget about the chairs tomorrow," Grammy added. "I want to be doubly sure you follow through with your commitment."

"The chairs will be delivered to the shop as planned. And, I'll even check back in once the shop owner tells me how long he'll need to complete the repairs."

"Thank you, dear."

When the conversation ended, Jackson made a goofy smile. "Wasn't it smart to get Knox lined up to take me to the qualifying swim meet? It'll give you time over the weekend to concentrate on work. No need to thank me for the big favor." He winked.

"Really?" Cate gave him side-eye in protest of the

unauthorized plan. His sheepish grin confirmed her point was duly noted. He quickly left the room most likely in search of friendlier vibes.

Cate redirected her attention to Knox. "Back to your uncle's surgery. It just so happens I'll be in Beaufort tomorrow morning, too. Grammy asked me to drop off some antique oak chairs whose cane seats need to be rewoven. I promised her weeks ago but never got around to it, so she set up an appointment for me to take care of it. Why don't I swing by the hospital when I finish taking care of business and keep you company?"

"Won't you be needed in the office?" His face lit up.

"I had already put in for a day off to settle in from the relocation, so no. I won't be missed. I've been craving Sally's Sunrise Biscuits and can pick some up to share. Nothing better than a flaky biscuit smothered in blackberry jam and a hot cup of coffee to pass the time." She made an offer hard to refuse.

"Sure, why not? I like how you think." He gently touched her arm.

The close proximity to the man who had once stolen her heart was anything but ordinary. Her chest rose and fell with rapid breaths. They were friends, had been in love, were supposedly going to be partners for life, but everything changed in an instant. "I'll need help with…" she spouted, unable to allow herself to get caught up in the moment.

Knox leaned in. "No problem. Just text me when you arrive, and I'll come to your car and grab the biscuits. Now I can't promise I won't sneak a bite. You'll have to take that risk."

"With marketing," Cate's serious tone didn't falter.

"For Guest Services. This is my dream job, and I want to do my best to start strong. I've a lot of ideas percolating, but my skill set is in customer service, and I'm not quite as savvy with the business side of things. I'd love to get some pointers from someone with experience…like you."

"Oh." He lifted his shoulder in a half shrug. "Sure. I got you. We'll have plenty of time to discuss your marketing issues tomorrow. Why don't you make a wish list of your top five priorities? That'll give us a good starting point. I'll schlep my tablet."

Before the moment could get personal again, she noticed Will and Eliza approaching.

"Party is dying down. Anyone interested in grabbing some ice cream at Island Scoop? I have a hankering for some butter pecan," Will confessed.

Eliza flirtatiously wrapped her arms around his waist. "You're always hungry. I'll share yours."

"I had a feeling you'd say that," Will teased, kissing the top of her head.

"As much as I'd like some peach ice cream, I think I'll have to pass. Tomorrow is going to be a long day. I need to get Uncle Charlie squared away before heading to bed. Next time?" Knox suggested.

"Yeah, man."

"Count me out, too." Cate acquiesced even though her sweet tooth disagreed. "Jackson and I are going to decompress in the air-conditioning and call it a day. I'm dead tired. Having my friends and extended family share in my joy is simply the best feeling. I can't thank you all enough." She fought back tears. "Jackson and I are heading out. Good night, everyone."

Chapter Five

The last thing Cate remembered before falling asleep in her cozy room at the beach cottage was the tender scene between the lead characters in the latest romance novel she was reading. Despite her busyness, she carved out snippets of time every day to escape to a fictional world. Cate's guilty pleasure was, and always had been, reading. Comparing Knox and herself to the characters was only natural for they shared a similar story—two lovers torn apart by unfortunate circumstances only to reconnect years later. If only life were that simple.

A shower before bed provided an extra hour of sleep. When the alarm clock sounded, Cate wasted no time. Today was not the day for her usual messy bun or high ponytail. Instead, she dragged out the expensive hair straightener from under the bathroom sink and plugged it in. Rummaging through a wicker basket filled with a hodgepodge of makeup, she applied enough to make it appear as if the sun kissed her skin. A matte rose lipstick finished the look. Grammy had an oft-repeated saying…a true Southern lady never left the house without her lips on.

Her outfit selection required some definite deliberation. If she veered away from her usual appearance, it might seem like she was trying too hard. Yet with her newfound confidence, she longed to up her game. Amidst the pile of clothing she had yet to sort and put away, a cute short skirt paired with a flowery blouse called her name. She traded her usual flip-flops for a pair of espadrilles to complete the outfit.

"Mind if I borrow your school tablet?" she had asked Jackson last night.

"Take it." He was all too happy to part with it, despite admitting to being behind on his summer reading.

Good thing she messed around with it before going to bed. She needed to make it seem as though technology was second nature, even if her tech skills were limited to logging customer reservations on the desktop computer at work. Her car was packed with the four chairs in need of an expert's touch.

Jackson had engineered the necessary space by flattening the backseat and gently arranging the heirlooms without compromising their structural integrity. He loaded the extra junk Cate had stashed in the car into a new laundry basket and carted it into the house to be sorted later.

By the time she hit the road, she was about thirty minutes behind schedule. Not her worst, but she certainly could improve. She spied two shrimp boats navigating the waters as she drove over the bridge to the mainland. Couldn't blame the vessels for her tardiness this time, only herself.

A new awareness crossed her mind as she listened to the car radio. Today she and Knox would be spending time together, thanks to some warm, flaky biscuits. Her insides were mushy for lack of a better word. Her conscience told her to be guarded, but her heart whispered…take a chance on love.

The minutes ticked by on the car's digital clock. If she hit any traffic near Beaufort, she'd miss her appointment by more than thirty minutes. Disappointing Grammy outweighed common sense. Full throttle on the gas pedal, she increased the car's speed, kissed her silver heart pendant, and made a little wish, hoping no police officers would cross her path for the next half hour or so.

Up ahead, a beat-up pickup truck was hauling scraps of lumber. The tailgate jiggled with every bump and pothole it ran over on the uneven state road. Cate attempted to pass it numerous times, but the steady stream of traffic kept her car in its lane.

A majestic egret caught her eye, drawing her attention away from the road. Within a split second, random pieces of construction material flew off the back of the truck, littering the highway. With nowhere else to go, Cate swerved to the right. "Oh, no." She rocked side to side in her seat, her tires rumbling over a broad piece of lumber. From her view, she couldn't tell if the wood contained nails or staples. She blew out her cheeks, thankful for keeping the car under control and not veering into oncoming traffic.

Ten miles later, Cate felt confident she had avoided a potential disaster. Just then, a *thump-thump-thump* sounded from the rear passenger side. The faster she drove, the louder it got. "Not now." Worried that it might be a flat tire, she slowed her speed. "I need to pull over." A glance at her watch made her stomach ache. At the rate she was going, she'd be lucky to arrive at the hospital before Uncle Charlie was wheeled out of surgery. She nibbled her bottom lip.

Around the bend, she spotted a grassy area with

plenty of room to survey the damage without being in harm's way. She flipped the turn signal and eased the car off the road and onto the shoulder. Carefully, she exited the vehicle and scooted around back. Sure enough—a flat tire. She lowered her head, covering her eyes with her hands.

In her head, Cate could hear her father's voice. "Changing a tire is a life skill. You never know when you'll need it." His sage advice garnered new meaning. Lamenting her lousy decision to ignore his words of wisdom, she weighed her options, sitting on a grassy knoll with her eyes closed. Her best ideas had a way of coming to mind when she gave herself some time to think.

Her moment of quiet meditation was interrupted by a car horn blaring. "What the heck?" Startled, she jumped up and sought refuge by the side of her car. From her vantage point, she spotted a tan-colored sedan coming up behind her. "Who's that?" She stayed put, nervous of traffic and strangers.

"Cate? Cate Ainsworth, is that you?" bellowed a gentleman's voice.

She spied an average size, middle-aged man with salt-and-pepper hair walking in her direction. "Mayor Sam. Am I happy to see you." She waved her hands in the air, relief washing over her.

"Nell, you were right." He beckoned her to join them.

Cate spotted Nell climbing out of the car, dressed in vibrant colors against her warm brown skin. "How did you find me?" she asked the tall, slender woman, elated to see a familiar face without much waiting.

"We were dodging pieces of lumber littering the

road. Sam swerved onto the shoulder to avoid contact," Nell explained.

"Wish I had done that," Cate groaned. "I was right behind the truck."

The couple offered a sympathetic nod.

"And today is our thirtieth wedding anniversary," Mayor Sam continued. "We're headed to Beaufort to celebrate with our daughter Adeline and her boyfriend." The couple locked gazes.

"Lucky for me you were headed in the same direction," Cate blurted, interrupting their brief moment of tenderness.

"Let's change this tire and get you on your way," Mayor Sam insisted.

While the mayor swapped the flat for the spare, Cate and Nell observed from a safe distance.

"You're awfully dressed up for delivering some antique chairs in need of restoration." Nell peered above the lenses of her black sunglasses.

"Grammy made a point of reminding me about the appointment and how the owner was doing her a favor. I'm trying to put my best foot forward." She tucked a stray hair behind her ear.

"Hmm…it wouldn't have anything to do with Knox being in town for his uncle's surgery, now would it?" Nell needled Cate.

Cate wasn't the least bit surprised that Nell, a close friend of Grammy's, didn't shy away from prying into her love life.

"The mayor and I had a rocky start, much like yours and Knox's," Nell revealed.

"How so?" Cate leaned closer.

"Suffice it to say, most relationships worth fighting

for have ups and downs. We eventually found our happily-ever-after. You will, too."

"All done," Mayor Sam shouted, pointing at the spare tire firmly in place.

Cate glanced at her smartwatch…an hour late to the appointment and counting. She hustled over with Nell following leisurely behind. Mayor Sam proved to be as handy with tools as he was politically astute with constituents.

"The tire will get you to Beaufort and back home *if* you obey the speed limit and avoid any hazards on the road. Think you can do that, Cate?" He wiped the grime from his hands with a stained rag.

"Yes, sir," her voice rang out with conviction. "Thank you so much for helping me."

"Now that you're taken care of, the missus and I will be on our way." He enveloped his bride in a side hug.

"I imagine you'd want to get to the hospital to see that man of yours, but you must drop off Grammy's chairs first. I'll give the shop owner a courtesy call from the car to fill him in on your late arrival. You, young lady, must keep your eyes on the road."

"Yes, ma'am," said Cate. "Happy Anniversary." Her voice trailed off, consumed by guilt that her offer of breakfast for Knox would be more like lunch.

****

Last night after Knox and Will volunteered to clean up the trash and recyclables at the end of the party, the two headed to the rear of the property toward the garbage cans and recyclable bin. Their conversation still weighed heavy on Knox's mind.

When out of earshot from the others, Will cleared

Jennifer Vido

his throat. "Have you given any more consideration to working for Purdey & Son? I realize you're focused on the surgery right now, but soon enough, Uncle Charlie will be on the road to recovery. If you think about it, the surgery has created a perfect storm of circumstances."

"How do you figure?" Knox's tone teetered between annoyance and curiosity.

Will flipped open the lids of the two garbage cans and stuffed the foul-smelling trash inside.

Meanwhile, Knox deposited the bottles and cans into the blue recyclable bin, the clanking sounds filling the space between them.

"Charlie, Cate, and I have major life changes going on right now. And, here you are after all these years, the one person who can help all three of us navigate those changes." His chest rose and fell.

"Sure, Charlie could muddle through this surgery without your help, but you would never have let him do that. Purdey & Son is on the verge of making a name for itself, and you have the ability to fill the missing piece. And most importantly, Cate is on the cusp of her career with the chance to become the person she's always dreamed of being. Who better than you to share your experiences and skills from the business world to get her to the next level? The way I see it, you belong on Gull Island right here, right now. This is your chance to make things better for the people you care about most. The question is...can you commit to sticking it out this time?" He jammed his hands into his front pockets.

Knox still wasn't sure if he had it in him to make the kind of commitment his friends sought. Sitting at the hospital in Beaufort, he gazed up at the gigantic monitor affixed to the gray wall displaying surgery status. He had been staring at it for the last hour and a half, tracking his uncle's progress. The surgery was estimated to take under two hours. If the display was accurate, his uncle would be finished right on time.

The waiting room was sterile and cold like in most hospitals. He touched a rather large, artificial plant that took up space in the corner near the only source of natural light, the irony not lost on Knox. The rest of the room was dark, even with the overhead recessed lighting illuminated.

A slight buzz in his pants pocket alerted him to a text. The older woman seated directly across from him paused mid-crochet, scolding him with a disapproving nod. Knox cracked a sheepish grin. The lady resumed her stitching, focusing on the task at hand. He slipped the phone under his sweatshirt, obscuring her view.

—*Running behind*—

The text from Cate read. Knox responded with a surprised emoji—he wanted to laugh at Cate's typical tardiness. But in reality, he couldn't wait to spend more time with her when, or if, she ever arrived. Text bubbles appeared as if she was going to explain, but she must have had second thoughts because they quickly disappeared. With time to kill, he closed his eyes and drifted off to sleep.

Someone tapped Knox on his shoulder, waking him from his impromptu nap.

A middle-aged nurse dressed in blue scrubs with cat-eyed readers hanging from her neck greeted him with a kind smile. "The doctor will be out shortly to discuss the surgery. As soon as your uncle awakens, I'll take you back to the recovery room to see him."

"Thank you, ma'am." He stood and stretched his long legs, sauntering over to the water cooler for a cold drink to moisten his dry throat from snoozing with his mouth open wide. Uncle Charlie teased him about it as a child, warning him a fly might land in his mouth if he weren't careful.

The sliding electric doors swished open and in scurried Cate. She held two takeout coffees with a tote bag slung over her right shoulder.

"Cate," he called slightly above a whisper. Seeing her peer in his direction, he exhaled a deep breath, relief washing over him. He motioned toward a vacant row of chairs.

"I owe you a cup of coffee. Black, if I remember correctly." She scooted next to him.

He nodded and welcomed the jolt of caffeine she handed him.

"Sorry I'm late. You won't believe what happened." Cate heaved a big sigh.

At that moment, the doctor entered the room. "Will the family of Charlie Price meet me in conference room 1A, please?" The older gentleman didn't wait for a response. He spun on his heel and headed toward the conference room.

"I could use an extra set of ears," Knox said. "I'm new at this caregiver role and now isn't the time to screw it up."

Without hesitation, she slipped her hand into his. "Let's go."

The gray-haired physician wasted no time getting down to business. "The hip surgery was a success. However, Mr. Price has experienced a minor setback. An irregular heartbeat warrants a visit to the cardiac floor before physical therapy can begin. The body reacts in unpredictable ways, especially for older patients with a history of health issues like your uncle. Better to be cautious than careless," the doctor advised.

Knox glanced from the doctor to Cate for clarification. It might have been years since he and Cate were a couple, but he hoped she could still read him like an open book.

Cate gently placed a hand on Knox's back. "Excuse me, doctor. You mentioned health issues. Would you mind being a little more specific? His nephew is from out of town, so he might not be up to speed on his uncle's recent health concerns."

Knox slightly nodded, his chin signaling to Cate that she had been right on the nose.

"Charlie has respiratory issues and circulation problems, all of which have been monitored and kept under control. The irregular heartbeat is cause for concern. He'll need to rest until we determine the cause."

"How will it affect his recovery from the hip replacement?" Knox asked.

"His physical therapy will be on hold. Usually we'd have him sitting up within a few hours, even taking a couple steps. For now, he will remain stationary. A precaution we must take." He crossed his arms over his chest. "He's scheduled for a battery of tests, all of which are standard protocol. As soon as we get the results, we'll have a plan of action. My gut tells me he's fine, but I need the results to confirm it." The doctor glanced over Knox's shoulder. "I promise to stay in touch. My surgical team needs me back in the operating room."

"Thank you for the update." Relieved by the news, Knox returned to the waiting room with Cate by his side. "I might be here for a while," he emphasized as the two sat in the same rigid seats they were in before.

Cate glanced at her watch. "Past noon already. Are you hungry?"

Knox raked a hand through his sandy-blond hair. "Starving," he admitted.

"I didn't make it to Sally's Sunrise Biscuits this morning, but I can scoot out right now and grab us some lunch. Just what the doctor ordered," she pronounced.

"You don't mind?" He hesitated.

"Be back in a flash." Cate grabbed her purse and headed toward the exit.

"Wait. I'll go with you." Knox didn't want to pass up the opportunity to spend some one-on-one time with her.

"The line is always long, but it moves quickly," Cate assured him.

Knox notified the woman at the reception desk that he was leaving the hospital for a little while and then joined Cate at the exit, placing a hand on the small of her back. "If anything changes with my uncle, the nurse has my number. She promised me I wouldn't be needed for a while. Ready?" He breathed in her familiar floral scent, her close proximity affecting him more than he imagined.

"All set." She matched his stride.

"I'm parked close since Uncle Charlie drove us here at the crack of dawn," he explained.

"Did you drive your truck?" Cate asked.

"Gosh, no. We borrowed a sedan. Figured Uncle

Charlie would rather slide into the seat than climb up with his one good leg."

"Smart choice, Nurse Knox," she teased.

They shared a mutual chuckle.

Knox used a map app on his phone to get them to the restaurant straight away. The midday traffic was unusually light, leaving them only time for idle chitchat.

Cate filled him in on the morning chair delivery. "The store owner promised to keep my tardiness to himself should Grammy ask if I held up my end of the bargain."

"I'm not the least surprised with the favorable outcome. You're resourceful in the stickiest situations and today is no exception."

The parking lot behind the building had one open space—just more good fortune shining down. The storefront space was narrow, making it difficult to step out of line to read the list of daily specials.

"Go ahead and use your charm to squeeze up ahead. Send me a text if the list is too long," Knox said. "I'll hold our place in line." Seeing as the majority of folks were preoccupied with their phones, Knox observed Cate infiltrate the line without being a nuisance.

She weaved through the crowd, tapping her fists together. "Scrap our original plan," she squealed within earshot.

"Are you saying what I think you are saying?"

"Creamy. Pimento. Cheese." The words oozed from her mouth.

On impulse, Knox wrapped her in a hug. "Just like old times," he spouted. The words slipped out before he could stop himself.

A frazzled young mother with two small children entered the store, brushing up against them. "Pardon me. Where may I find the restroom?" She tugged on Knox's arm, grabbing his attention.

He and Cate stepped aside, pointing her in the right direction.

Sheepishly, Knox decided to pretend his impulsive hug was solely because of his all-time favorite cheese concoction and not the urge to feel her in his arms again. He noticed how Cate inched forward with the flow of the line instead of facing him. Her subtle body language spoke volumes.

Now was not the time to discuss what, if anything, was happening between them. He had to keep reminding himself of his reason for being on Gull Island. Uncle Charlie needed his help. End of story. Yet the truth had more to do with winning her back. There. He said it...well, in his mind he did. The man afraid of commitment wanted to rewrite the past. But first, he'd need to figure out what was stopping him from moving forward. And then, he'd work backward to change it.

The hot, pimento cheese biscuits and sweet tea at Sally's didn't disappoint. Neither did the effortless conversation that flowed back and forth.

"Mind if I pick your brain about potential marketing ideas for Guest Services? I did what you asked and wrote down five specific areas of the business I could use some help with. I'm meeting with Kelsey tomorrow." She whipped out her brother's tablet and stylus, ready to jot down bullet points.

"Using me for my smarts, I see, and not my good looks," he teased.

Cate choked on a sip of sweet tea. "Glad to see you don't have any self-confidence issues. Some things never change."

He popped a morsel of the cheesy biscuit in his mouth and gave an exaggerated wink.

"While you savor a bite, let me run some of my ideas by you. Just nod yes or no," she instructed.

****

Nods of agreement and emphatic positive comments from Knox validated Cate's ideas. Her vision for Guest Services was becoming a reality.

"Cate, this is great stuff. You've done your homework and have a solid plan in place. I'm impressed."

"I appreciate your support, Knox. Your background makes you the perfect mentor."

Their conversation was spontaneous, and with familiarity more long-lasting than the lapse of years apart. Between the innocent flirting and impulsive hug, Cate had a sneaking suspicion Knox might be thinking he could just waltz back into her life without so much as an apology for the pain he had caused. If so, he was traveling down a road he had no right to be on...*or did he*?

On the short ride back to the hospital, she caught him peeking at her. Not simply a friendly glance but more of a longing, similar to the characters Abby and Beau in the book she was reading. Being vulnerable to a man who had broken her heart would require a tremendous amount of trust on her part, of which she was well aware. If only she dared to follow in Abby's footsteps and give her relationship with Knox a fighting chance.

****

The waiting room had emptied by the time Knox and Cate returned.

The attendant at the information desk waved him over.

Cate held back to afford him some privacy. The demeanor of the woman was difficult to decipher. Cate pretended to be preoccupied with her phone when in reality she was trying to lip-read. She could see the receptionist scribbling something on a sticky note which she handed to Knox.

He nodded a quick thanks and then headed over to Cate.

"Good news?" She wrinkled her nose.

"Yes and no. My uncle is still lying flat in a hospital bed in the cardiac wing. All the tests are negative, so the doc ordered two more. If those come back negative as well, Uncle Charlie will be moved to the orthopedic floor to begin his physical therapy," Knox explained.

"Gotta have patience at a time like this and hope for the best outcome." Cate encouraged him with a gentle pat on the back.

"I couldn't have said it any better myself." Knox rocked back on his heels, "The nurse gave me his room number. I imagine by now he's asking for me."

"Of course. Don't let me keep you. About time for me to get back to Gull Island, anyway. I don't want to risk running into any trouble with the spare tire." Cate adjusted the tote on her shoulder.

An awkward silence filled the air.

"Okay, so please let Uncle Charlie know I'm thinking of him." Cate lifted her chin to meet his eyes.

Knox narrowed the space between them, hesitating slightly and then gently kissing her on the cheek.

Cate closed her eyes for a brief second, breathing in the moment. Now was not the time or place to confront him about his intentions, purely out of respect for Uncle Charlie. As soon as she slipped behind the wheel in her car, Cate dialed Eliza. They rarely spoke on the phone, usually only by text or video chat. The call went straight to voicemail, not too surprisingly. If Cate had to wager a guess, Eliza probably had her phone on 'do not disturb.' The one time she wanted to hear her friend's voice, she got nothing but crickets.

The drive back to Gull Island was uneventful for Cate except for a phone call from the restoration shop. The chairs would require extensive work, most likely six weeks or more. Due to the backup of orders, the turnaround time would be close to eight. Grammy would not be pleased.

Rather than heading straight home, Cate opted to drop by Guest Services, hoping to catch Eliza before she left for the day. She parked the car in the circle and stepped up to the front door. A piece of white copy paper was affixed to the glass that read, *Closed. Please stop by Bait & Switch for Check-In.* Cate stared at the sign. Something big must have happened to have caused Guest Services to close, her mind imagining the worse.

"Catie-bird," called a haggard voice from behind. She perked up and smiled wide as Ol' Man Henry approached.

Chapter Six

A legend in the community, Ol' Man Henry was a living treasure on Gull Island. A sage, gray-haired man with weather-beaten skin, he couldn't help but get involved when tidbits were practically his calling card.

"Henry." She waltzed over, bestowing a proper hello.

"You missed Eliza by ten minutes or so," he explained. "On her way to Beaufort."

Cate smiled. "You don't say. Just came from that direction. I'm surprised we didn't cross paths."

Henry limped over to the wooden bench in front of the building and patted the seat next to him.

"I see your toe is still bothering you, Henry. Did you stop by Doc's and have him take a peek like I suggested?" She gazed at him down the bridge of her nose.

He exhaled a laborious sigh. "Doc McGuire has no business wasting time with an old man like me. God has given me one good foot to limp around on this island. Asking for two is greedy."

"Oh, Henry," she exclaimed. "One of these days, you'll listen to me. For now, let's get back to Eliza. Any idea why she drove to Beaufort? She was in charge of Guest Services today. Kelsey attended an off-site meeting late this afternoon, and I took the day off." Cate might have been recently promoted, but she was already thinking like a manager.

Propping his leg on the planter filled with local flowers, Henry jiggled his knee. "Let me think for a minute here. She was in a hurry. Said you were coming." He twiddled his fingers together. "Ah, I remember. Something happened to an artist on the West Coast. Unable to make the gallery opening tonight. They asked Eliza to fill in."

Cate tugged on his arm. "What great news. This could be her big break. But, she should have called or at least stayed long enough for me to cover." The conversation faltered as Cate got to thinking. This unexpected opportunity for Eliza would help her friend attain the goal she had been working toward for years. While Cate applauded Eliza's good news, she couldn't help but wonder what these big changes could mean for the near future in their personal and professional lives.

Eventually, Eliza would make a living in art and no longer need to rely on a part-time job at Guest Services for income, leaving another open position to fill.

The day would be coming soon, too soon for Cate's liking. Adjusting to change was never easy. "Thank you for the information, Henry. I apologize for cutting our visit short, but I need to get home to Jackson. He's preparing dinner for the two of us."

Henry adjusted his leg with his arthritic hand in preparation to stand. "Mary is expecting me home for dinner. Monday is fish taco night. Caught some dolphin fish early this morning."

"Sounds delicious. Please send my regards to your sweet wife." Cate offered him an arm to get up.

Henry's feeble legs held steady, sending him on his way back home.

Fewer than five minutes later, Cate strolled through the front door of the beach house, greeted by the strong smell of fish, wondering if she missed the memo about Monday being fish night on Gull Island. "You cook and clean?" she questioned.

Standing at the sink, Jackson used elbow grease to scrub a dirty pan. "Hey, sis," her brother piped up. "I made my version of shrimp burgers, spicy hot and warming in the oven." He placed the clean frying pan on the drying rack on the counter. "I'm leaving in five."

Cate slumped onto an oversized upholstered chair. "Whoa. Hold it right there, mister. Where are you off to in such a hurry?"

He tossed the towel at his sister. "Swim practice. Seven to nine tonight. Taking the golf cart, if that's okay."

"Get outta here before you're late. I'll finish tidying up the kitchen." She wadded up the towel and threw it in the direction of the laundry room.

Jackson headed to his bedroom for his wallet and house key. On his way out the door, he picked up the dish towel and deposited it in the laundry basket. "See you later. I won't be late."

"I'm counting on it." She winked. In the sudden stillness of the house, Cate let out a huge sigh, slumping back in her chair. First order of business was to straighten her bedroom and secure places for her belongings. Making quick work of hanging clothes in the closet, folding other items into dresser drawers, and moving scattered supplies into an orderly arrangement on her desk, she decided to change into a pair of short sleeve jammies. She opened one of the drawers she had just organized and grabbed the item on top, a silky pink-and-red-heart set she bought on clearance after Valentine's Day. The irony of choosing the love-themed pair wasn't lost on her. A sign? Probably not. Grammy would call it a coincidence. Either way, she was home alone, wearing romantic sleepwear with no boyfriend.

Wandering barefoot into the kitchen, she couldn't wait to try Jackson's culinary creation. For a teenager, he had more interest in cooking than she did at his age. Come to think of it, even now. When she and Knox were dating, he and her brother used to whip up some seriously good food together. She wouldn't be surprised if he opened his own restaurant on Gull Island one day. As expected, his sandwich boasted the perfect combination of spices and seafood.

What Cate liked best about living in the beach house was being alone, especially in the evenings. The night air had a way of relaxing her. The salty smell of the ocean calmed her mind and soothed her soul. With a library book in hand, she escaped to the screened porch and nestled into her favorite rocking chair. The quietness of the beach with the faint sound of the waves crashing on shore was the perfect setting for escaping to a fictional world.

Despite wanting to read her book, she kept getting sidetracked. The characters Abby and Beau had difficulty communicating their past hurts to one another. Abby needed to be understood, but Beau was focused more on moving past their troubles and starting fresh. Cate empathized with Abby to the point where she was getting frustrated by Beau's selfishness. Unable to separate fact from fiction, she tossed the book aside for another day.

Switching gears, Cate headed into her bedroom and took out a box of art supplies she stashed under her bed. Her mind clouded with too many moving parts, she decided to get busy on a new vision board. "Seeing is believing," Grammy often said, and what better way to accomplish a goal than to have a visual reminder? At the kitchen table, she cleared away the centerpiece to make room for her project.

The topic for the board didn't come easily. Deliberating, she brewed a cup of chamomile tea—part of her nighttime ritual. Filling the kettle with filtered water, she placed it on the stove and sparked the gas burner. Try as she might, she couldn't come up with an idea.

Back at the table, she flipped through a few magazines for inspiration. Not satisfied with what she was finding, she remembered having stashed a couple of new ones in her tote bag for the hospital. She ambled over to the comfy chair and retrieved them. On the cover of a working women magazine, she spotted a headline, *Work/Life Balance*. "That's it." Sipping her tea at the table, she began designing the board. Her new managerial position would entail long hours, which she was certainly not accustomed to working. Finding a work life balance was exactly what she needed to do.

Perusing magazines, she found pictures of women dressed in professional outfits to be used as the main focal points on the board. Working in a resort town didn't usually warrant a need for that kind of wardrobe, but she liked to think about 'what if.' She added a laptop, a pair of earbuds, and a functional tote as useful accessories.

The life part was a bit trickier. First, she asked

herself…what would her life be like? And who would be in it? Naturally, her mind drifted to Knox. Was he part of this vision? If she had asked herself years ago, the answer would have been an emphatic *yes*. After all they went through, the answer was still the same. Yes, they both had grown and changed, but maybe that wasn't as bad a thing as she first imagined.

Cate glanced at the clock displayed on the microwave. The time neared nine, which meant Jackson's practice would end soon. If she wanted to have a conversation with Knox, she'd better call him now. The words 'like old times' stuck in her head. What did he mean by that? Honestly, ninety-nine percent of the time they were together had been perfect. When Knox left town, things got a bit wonky.

Leaving the table, she retreated to the cushy chair. Of all the furniture in the beach house, this was her safe place. As a child, she'd nap in the chair after a long day in the sun. In her adult years, the chair was like an old friend—a welcome reprieve from a long day, a place to relax while reading a romance novel. Somehow, this simple piece of furniture provided peace, strength, and comfort. All three things she needed right now. Ready or not, she needed to find out the truth. Cate listened as the phone rang once, twice…

"Hey," Knox murmured.

One simple word that held much meaning. Where would this conversation lead them? "Hi, um, I was calling to check on Uncle Charlie. Hope I'm not calling too late." Cate sank deeper into the seat.

"No, no. Of course not. I was just leaving the hospital. Uncle Charlie will be reassigned to the orthopedic floor tomorrow. Doc thinks his heart issue was a fluke. No signs of distress, blockage, or irregular rhythm."

Cate let out a sigh. "You must be so relieved." She could hear the safety belt reminder dinging in the background followed by a loud click of the seatbelt. For as long as she could remember, Knox ignored the warning until someone suggested he buckle up.

"Uncle Charlie wants to get on with the physical therapy so he can come home. I don't blame him. He's been asking me to sneak him a shrimp burger."

They both laughed.

"Sounds like Uncle Charlie is on the road to recovery. I imagine you are exhausted from the long day," she surmised.

"I'm about thirty-five minutes from home. My head is hitting the pillow as soon as I crash through the door." He yawned.

"Would you like for me to keep you company on the drive?" Cate paused for a moment. "I wouldn't want you falling asleep at the wheel." She peered at the clock. For once, she hoped Jackson would be late.

"I'm in the middle of a podcast. I should be fine."

His words stung.

"Unless you've something on your mind," he added.

"What did you mean when you said it felt like old times?" Cate blurted. As soon as the words escaped her lips, she wished she could take them back. The conversation wasn't going as planned. Instead of dancing around the subject or seeing if maybe he would get the hint, she went full-on rogue. If only Eliza was around to role-play the conversation ahead of time. Too late now.

Knox didn't respond right away.

She listened to the *tic-tic-tic* of the turn signal through the phone line.

"I'm late, but I do have a pizza. Help yourself if you're still hungry. I'm starving," interrupted Jackson, holding the cardboard box.

With her attention sidetracked by the conversation, or lack thereof, she hadn't noticed her brother entering the cottage.

"I'm taking a shower before I eat. Be right back." Jackson motioned down the hall.

Shushing him, she waved him out of the room.

"Cate? Are you still there?" Knox asked.

For a brief second, she almost hung up. She had an out. Why not take it? But, the better part of her prevailed. "Yes, I am."

"I've never lied to you before, and I don't plan on starting now. Being with you is like old times. It feels right. We're in a really good place, Cate. Better than I could have imagined."

She cleared her throat, unsure of where this was heading.

"I'm only on Gull Island for a short amount of time. If you're open to it, I'd like to spend it with you."

"I hear you." Not exactly a resounding affirmation, but all she could offer on the spot.

"Ready for some pizza?" her brother shouted loud enough for Knox to overhear.

"Hey, you better take Jackson up on his offer before he eats the whole pie. Thanks for keeping me company today. I'll talk to you tomorrow. Good night, Cate."

"Good night, Knox." She ended the call and tossed

the phone on the side table. Cate appreciated Jackson's intuitiveness to brush over her serious call with Knox by monopolizing the conversation with his own news. She half listened, feigning interest when need be. Like the character Abby in her romance novel, Cate, too, was having difficulty letting go of her own hurt. Maybe the time was right to take a second chance on the one man who captured her heart.

****

Early Tuesday morning, Cate's adrenaline was revved up for the day. Before work, she had an errand to run. When she called Al's Autobody about the flat tire, the owner offered to squeeze her in only if she dropped the car off before the shop opened. As a favor to Cate, he'd patch the tire himself. If Al couldn't salvage it, he'd order her a new set. Otherwise, she'd have to wait until Wednesday afternoon for a technician to make the repair. The Tuesday schedule was already overbooked.

To make the morning run smoother, Cate fixed two lunches the night before and stuck them in the refrigerator. She even laid out an ironed uniform and tennis shoes for herself and a bathing suit and towel for her brother. When Cate showed up for breakfast, she was surprised Jackson wasn't already seated at the kitchen table. Were her lazy habits rubbing off on Mr. Punctuality? She smelled the brewed coffee waiting to be poured into her favorite Gull Island mug. On the counter, she spied a note written in Jackson's chicken scratch. *Early morning practice.* Nope. Mr. Punctuality was not following in his big sis's footsteps. She meant to ask him for a ride to work late last night before she fell asleep, but Knox occupied her mind.

In typical Cate fashion, she wasted her time weighing the pros and cons of being in a relationship, rather than taking care of her transportation issue. Without a ride to Guest Services from the shop, she'd likely be late again. Wondering if she and Knox had the potential to become a couple during his abbreviated stay was not a top priority…at the moment.

With little time to spare, she grabbed what she needed and set off. On the drive over to the garage, she considered a couple of scenarios on how to beat the clock and make it to work on time. If memory served her right, one of Jackson's classmates worked at the garage this summer. Fingers crossed he'd come in early for his shift and be willing to give her a lift. Second best plan would be to ask the clerk at the golf cart rental office for a ride. Surely one of these options would work.

At the stop sign, she flicked on her left blinker. Around the corner, the garage was completely dark. Not a light on, nor anyone in sight. Even the parking lot was empty. Cate bit the inside of her cheek. Hopefully, Al and Jackson's friend were not far behind. The clock was ticking.

Passing Bait & Switch, she noticed Knox's truck parked right in front. It never dawned that he might be around this time of day. She guessed Uncle Charlie was on the mend if he was here taking care of the business. Too bad she couldn't stop by and get an update on his uncle's progress or ask him for a ride. She didn't want to overstep or draw attention to her predicament.

Thankfully, the garage owner showed up shortly after Cate arrived. After handing off her car keys and finding out that Jackson's friend was scheduled for the morning shift, Cate paced back and forth, willing him to materialize. Unfortunately for Cate, he was not an early riser. Rather than waste more time, she headed over to the golf cart rental shop. As usual, a line of visitors new to the island formed out the door. Cate attempted to flag down one of the runners, but the guys were too busy fetching the carts to listen to her woes. Hands on hips, Cate closed her eyes and tilted her chin to the warm sky, pondering a solution. Something so simple and plain to see. If only she could figure out how to find it.

"Hello, Cate," shouted a friendly voice.

Cate opened her eyes and spotted Nell moseying toward her.

Dressed in cozy workout gear, she held a coffee in one hand and a set of car keys in the other.

"Ask and you shall receive" flitted through her mind.

"I hear you could use a ride." Nell jingled the keys.

"Where are you parked?" Cate hooked her hand in the crook of Nell's arm.

"Mayor Sam dropped me off on his way to a morning council meeting," Nell explained as they navigated the lot. "My car was at the garage for some repairs, ready to be picked up. Surprised to see the owner at that hour, I inquired as to why he was at the shop, and he mentioned your dilemma."

"If we hurry, I might make it on time." Cate clenched her fists.

The secondary roads were nearly empty, but the main roadway was clogged with tourists taking in the sights.

"No sense worrying about it now," Nell pointed out

kindly. "You'll get there when you do." She gently tapped her on the shoulder.

"Can't argue with logic," she muttered. Cate was destined to be late. "Hopefully, Kelsey won't be coming in today."

"Last time we met, you were charged with an important task. Tell me, dear. Were you able to drop off the chairs?" Both hands on the wheel, Nell's gaze never left the road.

Cate shared the story of her appointment at the antique restoration shop, including the disappointing news of the extended time required to repair the chairs. "To think a business exists just to restore old pieces into functional and praiseworthy chairs amazes me. Grammy insisted good craftsmanship was hard to find. After witnessing it up close, I can better understand why she chose this particular shop. The one-of-a-kind pieces waiting to be picked up appeared practically brand new."

"I imagine Grammy was less than pleased with the news," Nell surmised, thumbs tapping to the beat on the steering wheel, in time with the music playing softly on the radio. "But the most important thing is the chairs can be salvaged, given a second chance, so to speak. Not everyone has the ability to breathe new life into something in disrepair."

"True, but sometimes things are too far gone to be fixed." Cate had a sneaking suspicion their conversation was no longer about chairs, but something of far greater importance. Seeing as the car was moving at a crawl, she settled in for the ride. Cate perked up when Nell asked about her promotion. She took advantage of the perfect segue to get free advice concerning the office aesthetics. Nell had a reputation for having a keen decorator's eye, despite not having any formal training. As they neared Guest Services, the conversation focused on things more directly related to Knox.

"I understand Uncle Charlie will be heading to rehab tomorrow morning, which will free up Knox for the time being. Do you think you will rekindle your friendship or maybe more? The weatherman is calling for sunny skies the next few days. Perhaps you and Knox might take advantage of it."

The tone in Nell's voice didn't sound like merely a suggestion. Somehow, this woman sensed what was going on in Cate's mind, nudging her firmly into Knox's circle. "The island visitors will be happy with the forecast. I betcha the phones will be ringing off the hook. More excursions to book." Cate babbled, nearly tripping over her own words. The last person she wanted to talk about was Knox, not when she didn't even know herself what she wanted.

At the sight of Guest Services, she slowed her breathing to normal. According to her trusty smartphone, her shift started fifteen minutes ago. Not her worst to date, but a manager-in-training was expected to arrive for duty on time, if not early. Her relief elevated to panic when she noticed Kelsey's SUV parked in the circle. Not a welcome sight for someone with a long record of tardiness. Trying her best not to appear rude, Cate texted Eliza, asking if Kelsey was indeed at work.

—Yes—

The response punched her in the gut... Now what?

Nell parked the car in a prime spot in the circle.

Cate heaved a sigh of relief. "Thank you for the

ride."

"You're welcome, dear. And Knox?"

Cate pursed her lips. The clicking sound of the turn signal grew louder with every second. She understood Nell was coming from a well-meaning place, but she was late. Really late. Flinging open the proverbial door of opportunity, Cate exited the car. "I promise. I'll try," she shouted. "Thanks, again."

Quickening her steps, she entered the building with her head held high and her tail between her legs. This was not how she imagined reporting back to work after a day off, especially as the manager-in-training. Tuesday mornings were typically slow at Guest Services. By now, most visitors had found their vacation rhythm, beach-related activities in the morning and nature excursions in the late afternoon. At the front desk, she spotted Eliza engaged in a conversation with a young couple. Without interrupting the flow, Cate acknowledged her by waving a silent hello. "I'll be with you shortly," Cate informed a family with three children waiting patiently. On her way to the employee break room, she eavesdropped on Kelsey, talking on the phone.

"I'd prefer nonstop to a layover."

From the snippet of conversation, it sounded as if she was making travel arrangements. Throwing her belongings in the assigned wicker basket, Cate grabbed her name tag and headed back to the check-in desk to the family in need of assistance. All the while, she wondered where Kelsey was headed on short notice.

The family thanked her for arranging a dolphin boat tour and an alligator tour in less than ten minutes. When she suggested making a dinner reservation at a family-owned restaurant in Beaufort with a good reputation for catering to children with special needs, the parents were overjoyed. All it took was a phone call, and the table was confirmed for the following evening at six.

As Cate waved goodbye to the family, she noted Kelsey's broad smile. Personal attention to each guest helped Cate achieve the managerial position. Now if only she could find a way to work out the other kinks, most notably her repetitive tardiness.

Chapter Seven

At noontime, the office closed for lunch. Eliza hurried to the door to flip the *open/closed* sign before another guest crossed the threshold. "Did you pack a sack lunch?"

"Tossed it in the fridge," Cate replied. Cold pizza, a peach, and a bottle of sweet tea. And yes, I packed an extra slice." A simple gesture to help alleviate the elephant in the room. Cate wanted to talk to her friend face to face about yesterday's mix-up.

"Cate? May I see you in my office?" interrupted Kelsey.

Her boss's sharp tone left no room for debate. Cate stopped what she was doing and tentatively stepped into the well-appointed office that might or might not belong to her one day.

"Please take a seat." Kelsey gestured toward the chair in front of her desk.

In her mind, Cate debated whether she should offer an explanation for being late or wait for Kelsey to broach the subject. Despite the air-conditioning blasting from the window unit, Cate perspired, her hands clammy and her forehead damp with droplets.

"I'm not sure how to tell you this…"

Cate felt sick to her stomach. Please don't fire me, please don't fire me, played repeatedly in her head.

"My family needs me to come home sooner than

expected. I submitted my formal resignation this morning, effective Friday. We have three days to get you up to speed on the manager's position. I realize that when I offered you the position, I agreed to train you for the next month. Life sometimes gets in the way of best-laid plans, and your transitioning into this position is a prime example. Are you up for the challenge?"

By the time Kelsey finished explaining the extenuating circumstances, all Cate could do was nod. Her fear of being exposed for this morning's tardiness was long forgotten. Like it or not, she stepped into Kelsey's proverbial wedges, pinching herself to ensure she wasn't dreaming.

"Let's break for lunch. At two, we will begin your official training. In the meantime, I need to run an errand. If I'm not back when lunch is over, please feel free to familiarize yourself with this." She slapped a heavy binder on the desk. "The employee handbook outlines the responsibilities of the Guest Services manager."

"Yes, ma'am," Cate replied.

When the front door shut behind Kelsey, Cate beelined it for the breakroom. Only twenty minutes left to check in with Eliza before she had to reopen and be ready to accept guests.

"Hello, boss lady," Eliza greeted her. "I hope you don't mind me helping myself to your lunch. The pizza was delicious. Let me guess. Jackson ordered it."

"Kelsey is leaving earlier than expected. I've got three days to learn everything about the job," she blurted, her hands tightening into fists.

Eliza laid a hand on Cate's shoulders. "Three more days than you need. You've got this." She tossed her paper plate and napkin into the trash can.

"What happened at the art gallery?" Cate dared to ask, relaxing her hands.

"I've been biding my time until the perfect opportunity presents itself, and from the sound of it, this is a definite pathway into the Beaufort art scene," Eliza boldly professed.

"I'm surprised you chose to leave a note on the door rather than text me."

Eliza twisted the cap closed on her sparkling water. "I cleared it with Kelsey. I didn't want to interrupt your date with Knox." She lifted an eyebrow.

"Not a date, despite what you think. Wish I could've stopped by and seen your work on display. I hope your parents were able to drive over and make an appearance. Let me guess, and your mom cried tears of joy."

"She sure did." Eliza gave her the thumbs-up.

"You're not worried about how my manager title will affect our relationship, are you?" Cate jutted out her chin. "We might experience some growing pains, but overall, we're both satisfied with our current situations within the company. Right?"

"Absolutely," Eliza agreed. "I've never aspired to be the manager of Guest Services."

"Yes, but you rock at your job," Cate added.

"Thanks. I appreciate your understanding my current position is simply a stepping stone toward fully supporting myself as an artist. For you, all of this is your dream. We're both in our happy places."

Cate smiled, returning the compliment with a sweet hug.

After the lunch hour closure, visitors streamed into

Guest Services at a steady clip. Word spread about the scavenger hunt with a grand prize being a coveted personal tour of the historic lighthouse. Participants registered at Guest Services or Bait & Switch to pick up a Gull Island passport supplied by local businesses.

To drum up business on the island, Cate and Eliza encouraged the contestants to visit all seven stops. "Don't forget. Each team member with a completed passport will be entered in the drawing with the winners selected on Friday evening, five o'clock at the pavilion," Cate announced to the long line of guests.

The contest was scheduled to begin on Wednesday. Posters had been tacked up all over town to encourage people to participate. A goodwill donation of five dollars was recommended, but not required, and used to support the Lowcountry Conservation Fund. Between frequent summer guests and Mother Nature, preservation efforts were being ramped up to address erosion on the island.

"The stack of passports is getting low," Cate warned. "Do we have any more stashed in the back?"

Eliza nodded, continuing to help the summer guest leaning against the counter.

"Should've been prepared for the rush. What are we going to do now?" Cate muttered under her breath. The line in front of Eliza was six people deep, with no time to waste with guests clamoring for their passports. The contest began at nine the following day. "You hold down the fort. I'll head over to Bait & Switch and pick up an extra batch," she suggested. "I promise to be quick."

Once again, Eliza nodded her head.

Cate hopped in the Guest Services' golf cart parked

in front of the building, hands at ten and two, focused on getting there and back. Keen to the shortcuts, she managed to make it there in under ten minutes.

Like Guest Services, the place was packed, with not a space in the parking lot. Cate squeezed the cart into a makeshift spot near the front entrance, leaving the keys in the ignition to save time. She took the steps two at a time, barely catching her breath as she rushed through the front door. Inside the building, Cate caught sight of the crowded store, with vacationers scattered everywhere. With all the warm bodies in the building, the breeze from the nearby body of water did little to abate the stifling heat.

Cate scanned the crowd in search of Knox, his height making him an easy target to find. Crisscrossing the store to greet him, she spied him helping a gangly teenage boy ring up an order. The beads of perspiration trickling down his cheeks matched the sweat marks on his T-shirt. The South Carolina heat spared no one, especially during the hot summer months. "Excuse me." Cate butted in the line. "We're running out of passport books for the contest. Have any to spare?" she shouted over the crowd.

Knox jerked his head in her direction, eyes wide. "Absolutely," he answered. "I've got two unopened boxes in the office. Come follow me." He waved her over.

Those three words struck a chord for Cate. In the past, she followed him down a path with an unexpected detour. This time around, she preferred to be side by side. Inside the office, piles of hit-or-miss junk littered the space. "Did Uncle Charlie give his permission for this search-and-destroy mission?" She tiptoed around the heaps, careful not to disturb the mishmash of chaos.

"Please don't mention it next time you see him. The staff has been pitching in without me even asking, picking up shifts and helping when necessary. This is the only place in the store being neglected," he disclosed, stepping up onto a crate.

"My lips are sealed." She pretended to zip them shut with her thumb and pointer finger and then tossed the imaginary key over her right shoulder.

He grabbed the box of passports from the top shelf. "This is the last of them. Will's going to be thrilled when he hears the news."

"Perfect transition. I only have a minute or two, but I'd like to propose a barter agreement. You game?" she asked.

"Clock's ticking," he shot back, the box tucked firmly under his arm.

"The first project I'll be tasked with as manager at Guest Services is twofold—updating the website and overhauling our promotional material. Kelsey sent me an email about it yesterday so I'd have time to gather my thoughts before we formally discussed it. Oh, and I forgot to tell you."

"Tell me what?" he asked, shoving a crate of sundries aside to make room for her.

"Kelsey's last day is Friday," she stated matter-of-factly. "As in three days from now to be exact." She held up three fingers, driving her point home.

"Hmm, quite the task for you." He leaned against the doorframe, motioning for her to squeeze by.

"For us. Come walk and talk. Eliza is waiting on me." Cate headed back down the hall, her arm looped through Knox's.

"I'm guessing this is where you explain what I'm getting myself into. Am I right?" he asked.

Cate quickened her pace. "According to the grapevine, Purdey & Son has an upcoming marketing campaign with your name attached. Help me with my job, and I'll reciprocate. I'll take you to the best places on the island to capture photographs for your project. You'll be able to focus on caring for Uncle Charlie while I do your legwork."

"You and me? Working together?"

She caught a hint of surprise in his voice. "Is that such a bad thing?" They descended the front steps outside the building in tandem, racing toward her golf cart. "A win for both of us," she reasoned, climbing back in. "Whaddya say? You in?" She revved the engine.

"You drive a hard bargain, Miss Ainsworth." He leaned over and planted a light kiss on her cheek, slipping the box onto the back seat. "I'm in. Now get out of here." He laughed, double-tapping the roof of the cart.

Cate wasn't really sure how they would fit together, two very different people with seemingly divergent dreams and goals, but she was willing to take the risk to find out.

****

With only one bar of cell service at Uncle Charlie's house, Knox struggled to read the push notifications on his phone Wednesday morning. Uncle Charlie was scheduled to be released from rehab tomorrow meaning all the chores he asked Knox to complete needed to be done pronto. When another freelance job opportunity popped up in his inbox, he hit delete before reading with no regrets. If he wasn't thinking about his uncle, he let his mind wander to Cate. Her so-called barter deal was code for 'let's spend time together,' and he couldn't be happier with the arrangement.

Late last night, Knox wrestled with the pros and cons of rekindling a romance with Cate. When he arrived on the island, he initially rejected the idea of getting involved with her again, telling himself to stand firm despite the temptation. But now being in her orbit, he could not deny the magnetic attraction. Its intensity was hard to resist. He could refuse to see her, but his throat tightened at the implication. He was responsible for breaking her heart years ago. The guilt still haunted him.

His grogginess called for some caffeine. On the countertop, he noticed a haphazard sticky note affixed to the coffee machine which read...*don't forget to unplug*. Even from his hospital bed, Uncle Charlie called the shots.

On tap for today was a run to the hospital followed by a shift at Bait & Switch. Before he did either, he promised Will he'd stop by Guest Services for the Third Annual Island Scavenger Hunt kick-off celebration. Mother Nature even cooperated with sunny blue skies and a slight breeze.

Knox made a detour on his way to pick up Jackson. Will roped Cate's brother into working the registration table this year. Last-minute participants had an opportunity to enter the contest before the horn sounded, so extra hands were needed. Gull Island T-shirts were also available for purchase with all proceeds going to the island's conservation program. Knox planned to purchase one for himself as a memento of his visit. He craved the small-town vibe of the island, the familiar feeling of belonging to something bigger than himself shedding light on his present situation. If it weren't for Uncle Charlie needing surgery, Knox would have missed out on all of it.

Chatterbox Jackson didn't disappoint. Filled with enough energy for the two of them, his excitement was contagious. "According to Eliza, there are nearly two hundred fifty people registered for the scavenger hunt, not taking into account the others who will sign up this morning."

Knox steered the conversation away from the event. "Any updates on the swim meet? I meant what I said. If I'm free, I'll take you."

Jackson paused briefly. "I appreciate the offer, but my sister volunteered to take me this Saturday for the preliminaries, only a morning session. I need to qualify before I'm able to go on to the next round."

"No worries. If Cate is gung ho about it, don't let me step in the way."

"She said you can go, too," he offered, "but I'm supposed to make you think it's your idea, not hers."

In true form, Jackson's delivery fell short, but Knox didn't mind one bit. He liked what he said. "You can count me in. Let me know what time we need to leave. I'll drive the three of us."

Arriving at the circle, Jackson jumped out to man the table.

Knox circled around a few times before finding a parking spot. Most arrived by golf cart, but he didn't have that luxury since this was his first of many stops for the day. The registration table was situated right in front of Guest Services, guaranteeing he would bump into Cate at some point in the morning.

The sun slipped behind the clouds for a brief time, causing some attendees to glance skyward for a change in the weather. Knox's practiced gaze was drawn instead to the deer congregating near the hordes of people, nudging the summer guests for something extra to eat. Observing these beautiful creatures never got old. Stepping up to the sign-in desk, he was greeted by Will.

"Hey, man. Thanks for taking the time to be here. You've got a full plate, so it means a lot." Will fist bumped him. "And, please thank your uncle for me."

Bait & Switch was included as one of the seven spots to earn a stamp in the passport book for the first time. Will encouraged the local establishments to take advantage of the potential boost in revenue. With Uncle Charlie out of commission, Knox was banking on the contest to keep sales steady in his absence. "No problem. He was happy to do it. The shop is ready with flyers highlighting species of fish populating local waters. The back has a ten percent off coupon for a future bait purchase," Knox explained. "Actually, my uncle sprang it upon me the day I arrived. An impromptu deep dive into fishing, as he said. Learned more than I expected, while helping with the design."

"I have an idea. Why don't you register for the hunt? It'll give you some insight into the town and how it's changed since you've lived here," Will proposed.

"I couldn't agree more," chimed Cate from behind. "I have one lucky passport right here with your name written all over it." She waved it in the air.

"On one condition," he proposed.

"What's that?" Cate placed a stack of folded T-shirts behind the registration table.

"You're on my team." He drew in a breath in anticipation of her response, surprised at his own spontaneity.

Cate hemmed and hawed, playing right along, and then gave in. "Team Cate for the win." She handed over the passport.

"Whoa. Hold it right there," he chided her with a devilish grin. "You're joining my team, not vice versa. If anything, it should be Team Knox."

Cate's lips twitched upward into a smile. "Team Hip, Hip, Hooray."

"A nod to Uncle Charlie," said Knox. "I like how you think. We have four days to get all seven stamps. Doesn't leave us much time. We'll need to come up with a strategy." He moseyed over and casually draped an arm over her shoulder.

"Wish I could stay and chat, but I have a power meeting with Kelsey right about now. Think I can learn all I need to know in one day?" she asked.

He was distracted by the familiar scent of her shampoo. Some things never changed and for that he was grateful.

She nudged him in the side with her elbow. "Are you listening?"

He quickly recovered. "That's what on-the-job training is for. Get moving." He gently guided her toward Guest Services. "Last thing you want to be is late."

****

Approaching the hospital, Knox's demeanor instantly changed. So far, he had it easy by showing up at the hospital and keeping Uncle Charlie company.

The nurses took care of everything else. With his uncle's discharge looming, Knox needed to prepare for the next phase of recovery. Like Cate, he wanted to learn as much as he could today and then hope he had the wherewithal to get through the rest.

Knox recognized the low murmur of his uncle's voice before he entered his room. From the sound, Charlie wasn't pleased with what someone was telling him. Peering in the doorway, he met the eye of the nurse in charge, dressed in hospital-issued blue scrubs with a pair of cat's-eye readers resting on her head.

"About time you arrived," Uncle Charlie mumbled.

A throbbing vein on the nurse's forehead told Knox everything he needed to know. Someone in the room was being difficult.

"Your uncle has physical therapy two times today in preparation for his release. The therapist wants to see him climb up and down a set of steps before we clear him to go home. While I appreciate the fact there will be a bed for him on the first floor at home, steps are a mandatory part of the rehab program."

Knox didn't doubt this woman earned a reputation for sticking to the program. Negotiations were not an option. He eased into the chair next to his uncle's hospital bed. "Why don't I keep my uncle company for a bit?"

The nurse consulted her tablet. "The Occupational Therapist will be stopping by within the hour, as well. Please have your questions ready." Without another word, she was gone.

"Sorry I was late," Knox began.

"Cate rubbing off on you?" Uncle Charlie quipped, his sense of humor clearly intact.

"Registration started at nine for the annual scavenger hunt. Cate roped me into being on a team with her." Knox chose his words carefully.

"Catie-bird knows this island like the back of her hand. I'd say you two have a chance of winning," Uncle Charlie affirmed.

"That's not all."

Uncle Charlie waited.

"She is searching for help with the marketing and promotional side of her new job. Doesn't have any experience with it or at least not enough to make an impact. Made a crazy proposition. If I help her, she'll show me the best places on the island to take photographs. And Will's dad needs some help so I agreed to pitch in. Don't worry. It won't interfere at all with your recovery. I made that very clear." Once again, Uncle Charlie kept quiet which irked Knox. Unlike his father who had no problem voicing his opinion, his uncle remained tight-lipped.

By then, the OT was scheduled to arrive.

Knox stood to make room.

"Ask Cate on a date," Uncle Charlie whispered.

Knox did a double-take. He wasn't sure if he clearly understood what he heard, even though he wasn't the one with a hearing problem.

"A real date," Uncle Charlie clarified.

He certainly heard him the second time.

The OT entered the room and requested Knox leave to give them some privacy.

With a half hour to spare, he went to the coffee shop even though he wasn't hungry. Knox sat at a corner table and fiddled with his phone. When boredom set in, he made up his mind to text Cate. Asking her out in person would be the better choice, but lately they were running in opposite directions. Now via text made perfect sense before he lost his nerve.

First he added words, and then he deleted some. Attempted to be funny. Serious. Sentimental. Nothing sounded right. He could video chat her, but his insecurity had him circling back to a text. His uncle planted the seed. Now the time had come to see if it would grow. He kept it simple and hit *Send*.

By the time Knox rejoined him, his uncle was fast asleep.

The charge nurse stopped in with a brief update on his uncle's progress, including the tentative plan for him to be released in the morning. On her way out, she handed him a piece of paper with a To Do list written in his uncle's chicken scratch.

Seeing as the day was slipping away, he opted to take off for the pharmacy to pick up the medical equipment instead of sticking around. He was counting on the devices not requiring any assembly since he still had work waiting at Bait & Switch. Despite his growing list of tasks, Knox smiled to himself. A long time coming, nothing would stand in the way of his date with Cate.

****

With notebook and manual in hand, Cate sat opposite Kelsey in her office at Guest Services, scribbling as many notes as she possibly could in the margins of the manual. Making a concerted effort, she asked questions of clarification and jotted down important stuff in her notebook. Otherwise, their conversation was one-sided with Kelsey leading the charge. Midway through the lesson on employee hiring procedures, Cate's cell phone vibrated. Bored with the pages of government regulations, she slipped it ever so slightly from her pocket without Kelsey seeing. Widening her eyes, she couldn't believe what she read. Knox Price was asking her out on a date, by text. *Who does that?*

Chapter Eight

Romance readers like Cate set high standards for the art of dating. The number one job of a suitor was to woo a potential partner. Sending a text did not check off the box as far as she was concerned, nor did it come near to counting as a way to properly court a woman. Her exhale of frustration appeared unnoticed by Kelsey, who was droning on and on about some corporate rule. Cate considered Knox's present situation. Granted he was preoccupied with his uncle's well-being and freelance work for Purdey & Son. Cutting him some slack made sense, especially since she wanted to see if their so-called relationship had sea legs. The only way to find out was to rock the boat. She texted back.

—Yes—

"Do you have any questions about what we've covered so far?" Kelsey interrupted.

Feigning interest, Cate reread her notes. "Like you said, self-explanatory. In a pinch, I should find what I need in one of the divided core area sections."

"Have you worked out a marketing strategy? Competition is fierce in the hospitality industry." Kelsey removed her glasses and leaned back comfortably in her chair.

Now was the time for Cate to shine. Armed with the bullet points from her discussion with Knox, her previous research, plus on-the-job experience, her ability to sell the island to potential newcomers was being put to the test. "Service. In my humble opinion, service is how we will attract new people to Gull Island. Pre-arrival planning, concierge services, and guest manuals with each property rental."

"Go on." Kelsey planted a forearm on the edge of the desk.

"The majority of our listings are aged, needing updates. There are local contractors who come to mind who might help us in that department."

Kelsey's cell phone buzzed.

With a quick glance, Cate noticed her boss sent the caller to voicemail. "Our digital footprint is nearly nonexistent. That's the area I believe needs the most work," Cate stated in an authoritative tone.

"Tell me more." Kelsey leaned in.

"We need to find social media influencers to get the word out." She gestured with her hands. "Some target areas of the country might have never heard of Gull Island. It wouldn't hurt to explore getting a video channel. Think about the ways we could potentially use it. Explore hidden gems on the island. Feature weekly rental properties that have recently undergone a refresh. The possibilities are endless." Cate's enthusiasm boiled over.

"I remember you saying this was not your area of expertise. How do you plan on implementing these ideas?"

Cate adjusted herself in the chair, carefully choosing her words in response to Kelsey's valid question. "Funny you should ask. My old boyfriend is back in town helping his uncle recover from surgery. He's a whiz at marketing and offered his expertise."

The last part was a bit of a stretch, but Cate went with it anyway. Knox agreed to their arrangement. The how of it didn't really matter.

"Mixing business with pleasure?" Kelsey didn't cut her any slack.

Cate's cheeks pinked with embarrassment. Nothing popped in her head in response.

Kelsey stole a peek at her smartwatch. "I think we've covered enough for today. Judging from the noise outside, a crowd of scavenger hunt participants is searching nearby for stamps. That's something I'm going to miss about this place. Gull Island has a hometown feel three hundred and sixty-five days of the year." Kelsey packed her belongings.

Cate joined Eliza at the check-in desk, who was finishing with an older couple interested in making dinner reservations in Beaufort.

"I'm staying in tonight. Still trying to recover from the art show. I'm thinking of watching reruns of my favorite show. What about you? Have any plans?" Eliza asked when the office emptied.

A smile graced Cate's face. "As a matter of fact, I do. With Knox. A date."

"My, how the tides have shifted. I didn't expect this so soon. How did Romeo sweep you off your feet?" She wiggled her eyebrows.

"With a text." Even though she knew Eliza craved the deets, Cate kept it blunt and to the point.

"Really?" Eliza snorted a muffled laugh. "For someone so invested in romance novels, I imagine you'd expect much more. Amazing what love can do."

"Who said love? I didn't say love." She pressed a hand on her heart, shaking her head from side to side. "I said a date. He asked. I agreed. That's all. We'll see how it goes. End of story." As the words left her lips, Cate recognized this was not the end, but the beginning. Too many years had gone by without him in her life. "I'll take the reservation book to Bait & Switch," Cate volunteered.

"I was waiting for you to say that," her friend replied. "A piece of advice?"

"Always." Cate hugged the book to her chest.

"As much as you want a relationship with him, you're not the same Cate and Knox you were a few years ago. People change. Keep an open mind and heart."

With a quick nod to her friend's advice, Cate made haste to get out the door since Eliza was well along in her routine for closing up shop for the day. Climbing into the golf cart, Cate couldn't stop thinking about Knox. Relationships could be difficult. She could attest to that, but like Abby and Beau in her romance novel, maybe now was the right time to give love a second chance. Letting Knox back into her heart was a bold first step, a step she was ready to take. He made an overture, lame but well intended, and now she needed to respond in kind and see where this would lead.

****

Upon arrival at Bait & Switch, Knox checked the till. He was in charge of making the two daily bank deposits while his uncle was recuperating. Since the shop stayed open late, it warranted a mid-shift deposit. He could hear his uncle saying, "extra cash on hand only invites trouble."

Knox grabbed the green zipper pouch with the bank's logo printed on one side from underneath the counter. He withdrew the big bills from the cash drawer and filled out the deposit slip. Back out the door, he scooted to make the run. Taking the store's golf cart, he took off before someone recognized him. Now wasn't the time to engage in a polite conversation about his uncle's recovery with the customers. First, his chores must be done.

A tiny branch of the bank was located next door to the coffee shop, The Wise Owl. Since both establishments were open to the public for extended hours, it only made sense to be situated side by side. Unlike typical branches, this one offered a golf cart only, drive-thru lane.

Three customers were ahead of him in line, none of whom he could identify by name. He recognized the voice coming through the speaker as Nell's daughter. Getting in and out in a hurry would be tricky, but he was up for the challenge.

Knox placed the pouch in the extended drawer and waved hello to Adeline. The perky teller with light brown skin and dark curly hair waved hello and got down to business, much to his delight.

"I hear you're partnering with Cate for the scavenger hunt," Adeline dived in.

Knox slumped his shoulders. Just when he thought he was in the clear—caught red-handed at his own game.

"'Bout time you two tried again. Any special plans to get stamps?" She passed the pouch back through the slot.

Adeline was not making this easy. "News travels fast. I made a reservation at Blue Water Grille," he acquiesced, simply for time's sake. He tossed the pouch on the seat next to him.

"I'm counting on you two for the win." She winked.

The cart behind him tooted its horn. Thankful for an excuse to get away, he waved goodbye to Adeline and drove off, his confidence riding high in anticipation of the date.

****

Back at the shop, Knox caught sight of Cate slipping in the front door, and his heart skipped a beat. Though Cate was front and center, he still needed to check the bait refrigerators as the last item on his list. The wholesaler dropped off the weekly shipment on Friday mornings to prepare for the weekend rush. Orders were to be submitted by phone or online by Wednesday at six sharp. Miss the deadline, and no bait for the weekend anglers in search of a big catch.

He parked the cart and took the front steps two at a time. He cut over to the front counter and returned the pouch to its rightful place. He scanned the store and noticed Cate talking with a woman close in age. Happy to see her occupied, he raced up the staircase. The refrigerated coolers were lined up below the windows overlooking the water. He greeted a few regulars discussing where the fish were biting that day. Wasting no time, Knox checked the inventory then rushed back downstairs and placed the order. His primary responsibility as a teen, he completed the task in expert time. Time to change into a fresh shirt, spritz some body spray, and scoop up his date.

Knox found Cate in the same spot, gabbing with the same girl. As he approached, the two said their goodbyes. Knox couldn't have timed it any better if he tried.

He traipsed over and placed his two hands on her petite shoulders. Her energy instantly radiated through his body. He hadn't realized how much his soul missed her. "Money deposited. Bait ordered. Ready when you are."

"I'm still dressed in my work uniform, silly." She tapped him on his nose. "Mind if I use the back room to change?" She held a small nylon bag in one hand and a pair of wedges in the other.

"Go right ahead. Did you remember your passport? We have places to go and people to see. Let's win this thing." His raised voice and matching fist in the air caused heads to turn and stare.

Cate grinned. "I see your competitive streak is back in full swing, but you might want to tone it down a notch or two."

"They're just jealous because we're gonna win. Our reservation is for six at Blue Water Grille. We need to get moving pronto. On the way back from dinner we'll make a side-stop to pick up another stamp for our passports. If all goes as planned, we should have three before the night ends."

Playfully Cate saluted him like a soldier, which triggered a belly laugh, and then sashayed to the back to change.

While waiting, Knox sent his uncle a text, reassuring him the bait order was placed on time and that he would be at the hospital bright and early tomorrow morning for the discharge. Almost immediately, he received a string of emojis with a hodgepodge of unrelated characters...an avocado, a magic eight ball, and popcorn. He struggled to figure out the cryptic message. Ever since learning about digital images, Uncle Charlie used them obsessively. No more words, just so-called funny pictures. If only Knox could gaze into the magic eight ball to see whether or not he and Cate would have a future. Maybe Uncle Charlie was onto something, after all.

At first, Knox didn't notice Cate heading in his direction. What caught his eye was the flowy floral dress hugging her in all the right places. When he lifted his head to gaze at her face, he caught sight of the upward curves of her warm smile he remembered so well. "Before we leave, let's get our first passport stamp. C'mon. Let's go learn about local fish," Knox suggested, fumbling for her hand. He led her over to the opposite corner of the store dedicated to the contest.

Uncle Charlie kept the scavenger hunt decorations to a bare minimum. "Fewer to take down at a later date," was his uncle's terse explanation.

Knox heeded his uncle's instructions, tacked up only the free promotional posters supplied by Will on the walls, and arranged neat stacks of flyers on a makeshift counter. One of the shop's summer helpers was tasked with stamping the contestants' passports and passing out the flyers. Guilty for jumping ahead in line, but with a dinner reservation looming, Knox did it anyway. A newly designed Bait & Switch flyer and after two quick stamps on their respective passports, out the door they exited. "One down, six to go," Knox pointed out. He placed a hand on the small of Cate's back, guiding her toward the golf cart.

Cate perused the Bait & Switch flyer. "Not your typical scavenger hunt handout."

"You like?" he dared to ask, sliding next to her in

the cart. He flipped the ignition switch, easing out of the parking spot onto the public road.

Cate examined it more closely. "Very upscale if you ask me. The bold lettering at the top is perfectly in proportion to the smaller print. A school of designer fish is swimming under the heading. Did Uncle Charlie source this out to some froufrou company on the Internet before his surgery?"

"Kind of." He tilted his head.

"I don't see a design logo anywhere on the back. I definitely need to use this company for my new marketing material for Guest Services. Think I can finagle a discount? I can't blow my entire budget on my first project." She winked, leaning in to rest her hand lightly on his leg.

Knox kept his gaze focused on the road. "If you play your cards right, I think that might be arranged."

"Really? Do you personally know the designer?"

The gentle squeeze of her hand told him she was on to him. "Glad you approve. My conceptual design and verbiage were created under pressure. Uncle Charlie strong-armed me into doing it."

Cate sat upright, gently taking back her hand. "Good idea on my part to barter services with you. Outstanding piece of work, mister."

"Wait 'til you see my other talents." And he left it at that.

****

The Blue Water Grille was nestled in a remote area of the island near the marina. Cate kept tabs on its construction when it began two summers ago. Purdey & Son designed the structure and built it using repurposed wood sourced from the island. She only visited once, at the grand opening with Grammy, and the mouthwatering meal lived up to expectations. Tonight, she had her heart set on she-crab soup. The locals raved about the menu specialty, tender Atlantic blue crab meat and crab roe in a rich creamy base with a dab of sherry.

The parking lot was jammed with carts and cars alike. Cate spotted a diner backing out of a spot, making room for Knox to park close to the door. With five minutes to spare, they leisurely made their way to the hostess stand walking hand in hand into the bustling restaurant.

"Price, party of two," Knox announced.

Liking the sound of it, Cate smiled.

The young woman staffing the desk scrolled through a tablet. "Your table is ready. Please follow me." She grabbed two menus and then led them to their seats.

Cate was wowed by the staff's efficiency. So far, the evening was going smoothly. Once seated in the two-person booth, she observed her surroundings. "The restaurant's coastal decor is quite an eclectic mix of beachy elements." She admired a whimsical nautical paddle mirror hanging on the wall next to their table. An eye-catching chandelier constructed with various shades of white seashells dangled from the ceiling.

"This will be the second scavenger hunt stop. After dinner, we'll head out for another stamp, destination to be determined." Knox removed his passport from his pants pocket.

The server stopped by the table and introduced herself, handing each a fancy blue menu with the restaurant's signature ocean wave sketched on the front.

"What would you like to drink?"

"Water with lemon for me," Cate requested.

"Same, thank you." Knox nodded.

The server recited the daily specials, all of which originated from the sea. "I'll give you a few moments to peruse the menu." She stepped away, checking on the guests at an adjacent table.

Knox inched closer. "I hope you're in the mood for seafood."

Cate laughed. "I'm eyeing the she-crab soup for an appetizer and maybe shrimp and grits for my entree."

"You can't go wrong with shrimp and grits," he agreed. "The fried flounder featured in the menu here"—he pointed to it—"served with slaw and hushpuppies sounds delicious. I think I'll go with that."

As if on cue, the server reappeared and took their orders.

With the food choices squared away, Cate was anxious to fill Knox in on her conversation with Kelsey. "I made it through the day's training, one step closer to being in charge." She beamed.

"I'm sure Kelsey was blown away by your innovative ideas and even more confident she picked the right person for the job. From our brainstorming session, you were already way ahead with your creative thinking. Too bad I won't be available to troubleshoot in case anything goes haywire during your first days as manager. I'm still picking up the slack at the shop, plus Uncle Charlie is scheduled to be released tomorrow."

On the table, Cate rested a hand on top of his. "I bet you'll feel more comfortable about the whole situation when you and your uncle are under the same roof. No more driving back and forth to Beaufort."

Knox nodded. "Honestly, my schedule is going to be jam-packed. Possibly the only free time I'll have is in the evening, once Uncle Charlie goes to bed. Between helping with the shop and taking him to physical therapy, my time is not my own right now."

Cate closed a hand on the water glass, buying time to choose her words carefully. From what he was saying, he sounded like he was withdrawing a little. The whole point of this date was to figure out where their relationship was headed, and communication would be a big part of that. She decided to take a different approach. If he was withdrawing, the game would be next to go. "What about the scavenger hunt? We only have until Friday afternoon at five."

"Plenty of time to get the rest of the stamps. Speaking of which, I'll text you a game plan tonight. If we knock out about two a day, we're golden," he explained.

The server interrupted, setting their first course on the table. "Please be careful. The cups are hot. She-crab soup for the lady and a cup of gumbo for you, sir. I didn't mean to eavesdrop, but are you participating in the scavenger hunt?"

"Yes," they replied in unison.

Well, that's encouraging, Cate mused.

"Great. The beautiful red roses centered on the table have been donated from Petals. They're yours to take when you leave."

"I hope they aren't red flags in disguise," Cate muttered under her breath.

"Excuse me?" the blonde-haired server questioned.

"Nothing." Cate didn't even bother with a plausible cover. "Please continue."

"A last-minute bridal shower cancellation metamorphosed into a business opportunity of sorts. All the flowers on the tables were donated to scavenger hunt participants. You are in luck tonight. Oh, and don't forget to take a selfie down by the boats in the marina and post it on social media with #petals. Your photo might get picked to be featured on their website. And as an added bonus, the florist's business card is tucked inside with a ten-percent-off coupon for a future order."

With her insecurities resurfacing, Cate could only hope Knox might find that coupon handy.

"The hostess will be happy to stamp your passports on your way out," she added.

"Thank you. We appreciate your telling us." Cate minded her manners. The server wasn't to blame for the date going slightly sideways.

"So where did we leave off?" Knox picked right back up.

"Jackson mentioned you were free on Saturday and volunteered to drive us to his qualifying meet," she mentioned, eyes narrowing.

Knox paused with a spoon midway to his mouth. "Always have time for him. It'll be fun. All three of us. Just like it used to be."

His answer was what she needed to hear…just like it used to be. Maybe she was nitpicking his words tonight, instead of taking them at face value. He would be busy with work and his uncle, she reasoned. And he said he was coming up with a plan to get all the stamps for the hunt. Even if their schedules weren't in sync right now, it didn't mean they wouldn't be in the near future. Cate decided to make the best of the situation and concentrate on getting to know, once again, the man sitting opposite her at the table. Knox had broken her heart not too long ago, but he initiated this date, so he must be interested, right?

In no time, they were laughing together as they reminisced over teenaged antics. "I'll never forget when you and Will served me ice cubes with ants inside." Cate rolled her eyes. Crisis averted.

Full from their cooked-to-perfection meal, the two passed on dessert. Despite her earlier mood, Cate gladly accepted the flowers from Knox's hands as they left the table and even suggested taking a selfie to post on social media. With his hand on the small of her back, he led her toward the marina. The subtle gesture erased some lingering doubts.

Others in the after-dinner crowd took advantage of the magnificent views and cool night air by the water. Cate snapped a few pics and asked permission to post before he changed his mind.

"Absolutely," he replied. "We've got to do our part to support small businesses. Plus, we make a good pair."

Cate couldn't agree more.

"Before we call it a night, mind if we stop by The Wise Owl? I'd like to get one more stamp before the day is over. I'm dedicated to winning the scavenger hunt, if you couldn't tell."

"Actually, I could use a relaxing cup of tea before bed. Let's go."

The coffee shop was doing land-office business. All the inside tables were taken, and the limited seating out front was filled, too.

"I'm happy to stand in line," Cate offered.

"Why don't you hover by the outside tables to grab

the next available one instead? Your height is a little less conspicuous," he teased.

"Good idea." She handed him the passport.

"Great minds think alike," bellowed a familiar, strong male voice.

Cate was pleasantly surprised to see Eliza and Will coming in her direction.

"Aren't you tuckered out?" Cate teased her best friend within earshot.

Eliza gave her a hug. "Much too beautiful of a night to stay indoors. Will convinced me to grab a cup of tea and a stamp, of course." She produced her passport for all to see.

"I can't have my girlfriend falling behind in my own game," Will teased. Lacing his hand in hers, he gently kissed her cheek.

"That would not be good," Knox agreed. "C'mon. Let's get in line before they close."

Will headed inside with him, leaving the girls to find somewhere to sit.

Two couples rose from a four-top to the right of the front door.

On cue, Cate hustled over. "May I have your table?"

"It's all yours," replied a tall gentleman, dressed in Bermuda shorts and a short-sleeved, sky-blue, linen shirt.

Eliza trailed at a polite distance. "Spill it. How's the date going?" Once seated, she wasted no time.

Cate shared the string of selfies on her phone. "The restaurant was hopping with customers. The food is by far the best in town."

"Fast forward, please." Eliza squealed, resting elbows on the table and chin on fists. "Who cares what you ate! I want to know how you felt."

Cate drew herself up a little taller. "Where should I begin?"

Chapter Nine

Cate closed the gap so others wouldn't overhear. "It started off fine, took a sudden dip, and ended on a high note. Word to the wise, I need to stop overanalyzing and go with the flow."

"Hallelujah. Follow your heart and not your mind. I've been telling you that for years." She wagged a finger.

Cate rolled her eyes. Eliza didn't mince words. That's what made her the best kind of friend. They didn't have enough time to discuss what caused the date to take a nosedive because the line cleared out faster than anticipated.

The guys joined them at the table with drinks in hand.

"Three down, four to go," announced Knox. "Team Hip, Hip, Hooray is off to a good start." He tossed both partially stamped passports onto the table.

Will patted his friend on the back. "I had no doubt you'd be a contender for the big prize. What's on tap for tomorrow?"

Sipping her tea, Cate was curious about Knox's plan and if it included her.

"Off to the hospital at the crack of dawn. Uncle Charlie's nurse indicated he probably wouldn't be ready to leave until after the doc finished his rounds, but not worth sleeping in. My uncle will be blowing up my phone, wondering where I am if I show up past eight."

They all laughed.

"The freezer is full of casseroles from friends, so at least I don't have to worry about feeding him or me. I have rotisserie chicken, mashed potatoes, and a salad for tomorrow's dinner. Not sure how much he'll actually eat, but I wanted to have his favorite meal ready to serve."

Cate sat there and took it all in. For someone who claimed to be noncommittal and afraid to set down roots, he sure seemed like he was making himself at home. She could get used to having Knox around.

Will raised an eyebrow at Eliza.

Cate detected his facial cue—something important was about to go down.

Eliza nodded ever so slightly, giving him the go-ahead.

"So, my dad has a few ideas percolating in his head about the rebranding campaign he'd like to launch," he began.

"Rebranding or marketing? Two very distinct things. Which is it?" Knox lifted his hands in the air.

"A little bit of both. The company's niche is building homes for generations of Southern families. With more Northerners moving into the area, he'd like to establish himself as the building expert on Gull Island." Will delivered his best pitch. "Think you'd be up for hearing him out? Maybe give him your two cents on the marketing strategy?"

Knox fiddled with the plastic coffee lid. "Let me think about this and get back to you. Is there a timeframe I should be aware of?"

Will draped an arm over Eliza's chair. "I think he is hoping to forge ahead in the next week. Now is the time to strike with summer guests on the island with money to invest."

"Duly noted." Knox crossed his arms over his broad chest. "Let me mull it over for the next day or so and get back to you with my initial ideas. Then we can talk about specifics."

"Perhaps after work tomorrow, Cate might take you over to the sections of the island that are primed for new construction," Will continued with his gentle plea. "Snap some photos. Get a feel for what we're trying to accomplish."

Eliza kicked Cate under the table, girl code for your chance to talk.

"I don't mind at all," she piped up. "Jackson has swim practice, anyway. It'll give me something to do. And if we time it right, we could catch the sunset. Get another stamp."

Knox hesitated, for a moment. "If Uncle Charlie is stable and feels comfortable with me leaving him, I'll do it," he blurted.

Pleased with the progress made on all fronts, Cate suggested the friends part ways. She had high hopes for where her relationship with Knox was heading. Despite her trepidation, she realized everything was falling into place.

As they paralleled the beach driving to Grammy's cottage, Knox pointed out the tide rushing onto the shore depositing seaweed and shells.

Cate silently wished his love for her matched the incoming tide, deep and unstoppable.

****

Knox's internal clock woke him abruptly at six-thirty, ready for the busy day ahead. No lingering in his childhood bed at Uncle Charlie's house checking emails or texts. A full day awaited his prompt attention. Late last night, he fell asleep dreaming about Cate. Try as he might, he couldn't get her off his mind. Things were getting real.

Rummaging through his uncle's dresser drawer, Knox found a navy pair of soft drawstring sweatpants to pack for the hospital. The discharge nurse indicated the need for lightweight pants he could easily slip on and off. No bending or reaching for Uncle Charlie for a short time. From a shelf in the closet, he grabbed a grayish-blue Gull Island T-shirt from a stack. It might not be what his uncle would have selected himself, but at least Knox picked practical clothes for his circumstances. In the garage, he found a pair of slip-on tennis shoes, even though his uncle was more of a flip-flop kind of guy. For now, these shoes would have to suffice.

Knox had never been the type to keep a list of things to do. In his professional life, he added all his appointments and reminders to his online calendar. His uncle, on the other hand, was old school. He used the free wall calendar from the bank as the keeper of his days. Naturally, when the topic of therapy and doctor's appointments arose, Uncle Charlie insisted Knox take the calendar hanging on the kitchen wall to the hospital. No sense talking to him about using his phone's calendar app instead. This was a prime example of learning to choose his battles, especially since this was only the beginning.

Armed with all the necessary items, Knox left the

house. Running over the day's schedule in his head, he sighed, his responsibilities weighing heavily on his mind. More people than he realized were counting on him. First priority was his uncle. So far, preparedness for his arrival home was spot-on. Time would tell how good his caregiver skills would be. He anticipated the hardest part would be convincing his uncle to take it easy.

Agreeing to take part in the scavenger hunt with Cate as his partner was a spur-of-the-moment decision. Any excuse to get closer, he was willing to take. Bartering for his professional mentoring services, though, held the potential for burdening him with undue stress. He warned her ahead of time that his schedule would be too jam-packed to help her at first. He sensed her disappointment at the time, but he couldn't just leave her in the lurch.

The freelance work at Purdey & Son intrigued him twofold. He thrived when professionally challenged, and this particular assignment was definitely out of his comfort zone. The attractive part of the whole thing was having a plausible excuse to see Cate—anything to help regain her trust. His fear of commitment was no secret; after all, he had left her behind once. Yet if he expected her to give him a second chance, certain things would need to change.

At the hospital's entrance, he passed through the gate and grabbed a ticket from the parking kiosk. In the brief delay before the bar raised, he checked the clock on the dashboard. Not yet eight o'clock. At least he made it with plenty of time to spare. This called for a quick stop at the hospital coffee shop. With his mind preoccupied this morning, he forgot to make a to-go cup on his way out the door.

The shop was small, with barely room enough to serve a handful of people en route to the visitor's desk. Standing in front of the counter was Ol' Man Henry. Not the person he expected to see in such a place. He rarely ventured off the island. "Good morning, Henry." He tapped him lightly on the shoulder.

Henry finished pouring his cup before acknowledging Knox's greeting. "Good day. Here to pick up your uncle, I see." A polite smile crossed his weather-beaten face.

Knox grabbed a paper cup from a tall stack. "Yes, sir. He finally gets to come home. And, you? What brings you to Beaufort?"

Henry mumbled to himself.

A light flicked on in Knox's head. "He asked you to come, just in case I didn't make it in time. Am I right?"

Henry hemmed and hawed, babbling about the price of coffee these days. "Guilty as charged."

"I see old habits are hard to break. Cheers." Knox tapped Henry's disposable coffee cup with his own.

"Mind if I join you?" Henry asked tentatively.

"Might as well. You're already here." Knox stepped aside to allow Henry to lead the way.

On the elevator ride to the fifth floor, Henry greeted Dr. McGuire, a fit, medium height man from Gull Island. "My big toe has been bothering me for weeks, Doc. I surfed the Internet. I'm pretty sure I have gout."

"Why don't you give my office a call? I'll squeeze you in for a next-day appointment," offered the general practitioner.

Knox marveled at yet another perk of living on a small island—running into someone at the right time. Upon entering his uncle's room, Knox was blinded by the sunlight streaming through the open windows. Charlie was propped up in a chair with pillows on each side, talking with the slim discharge nurse with auburn hair. When the matronly woman made eye contact with Knox, the visible tension in her shoulders subsided. Almost time to relinquish her duties and let family step in.

"You made it," Uncle Charlie bellowed.

Knox and the nurse exchanged a sympathetic shrug. This job he signed up for would test his patience and resilience. If this morning was any indication of what he could expect, he had his work cut out for him and then some. Lately, Knox found himself taking a breather when all around him was uneasy, like in his present situation. Simply directing his own steps gave him a much-needed boost of confidence, keeping him grounded and well prepared for the task at hand. "Want these?" Knox held the drawstring bag with his uncle's clothes. "I bet you're itching to get out of the hospital gown," he joked.

Henry stayed on the periphery, sticking close to the door. He mentioned his dislike for hospitals on their way to the elevator.

His being there spoke volumes about his friendship with Charlie.

Uncle Charlie acknowledged his buddy with a wave. "Sorry to make you come all this way for nothing."

"As I told you over the phone, I have business in town today. No big deal," Henry explained.

"And, he managed to get an appointment to see about his toe," Knox added. "I'd say we've had a good morning all around."

The nurse glanced at the clock on the wall. Wasting no time, she rattled off discharge orders highlighted in the paperwork.

Knox raked his fingers through his hair, a habit he had since childhood. The nurse seemed anxious to finish her duties, spewing her words at a dizzying pace. He could tell his uncle was half-listening by the disinterested demeanor. Knox wasn't sure whether he was just dazed by the pain medication, or if he simply wasn't interested in what the woman had to say. Knox took what she said seriously. The first few days would determine how well recovery would go. If Knox could get his uncle on board, everyone would benefit in the long run.

"Transport should be here within thirty-five minutes to wheel your uncle to the pick-up circle, so please get him dressed and ready to go. Your paperwork has a twenty-four-hour phone number listed, in case you encounter any difficulties. Follow the instructions and you won't need it. My pleasure taking part in your recovery, Mr. Price. Be well," she said with a half-smile

Knox and Charlie thanked her simultaneously. At least Charlie's manners were still intact.

"I'll step out in the hallway while you get dressed," Henry volunteered.

"You'll do no such thing," Charlie insisted.

Henry obliged by staying where he was, his back to them and out of the way.

Knox removed the clothes from the bag and laid

them neatly on the bed one at a time. He leaned over and started untying the hospital gown from the back. "If you don't hurry, the transport person will pass by and you'll be stuck here all day." That was all Charlie needed to hear. Without fuss, he transformed into a compliant patient in search of a one-way ticket out of there.

"How was the date?" Charlie redirected the conversation.

At the mention of gossip, Henry clumsily moved closer to the bed.

"The Blue Water Grille far exceeded my expectations," he began. "Cate raved over the shrimp and grits."

"We don't have much time, son," Uncle Charlie butted in. "Thumbs-up or down. Keep it simple. Ouch," he exclaimed. "Stay clear of my sutures."

"You were right. Asking Cate on a date was a good idea." Knox shook his head.

Uncle Charlie muttered "told-you-so" under his breath.

Ol' Man Henry cracked a smile.

"Swap keys with Henry," Uncle Charlie ordered. "No way I'm climbing up into the truck with this new hardware."

Knox removed the keys from his pocket and handed them over. "Good point. In my rush to get everything ready, I totally forgot about that."

"Rookie move," Henry teased.

A *rat-tat-tat* on the door signaled they needed to leave.

Knox dressed Uncle Charlie without fuss. The last thing they needed to do was collect the discharge papers and take-home meds, both of which were stuffed in the hanging pocket on the wheelchair. Knox left Henry to see to it that his uncle made it down to the circle for pick up. "Leaving," he said with Henry's keys and parking ticket in hand on his way to retrieve the car.

When Knox drove up to the circle, he quickly located his uncle among the others ready for departure. Right before his very eyes, Henry popped a wheelie over the curb with his uncle hanging on to the wheelchair for dear life. The raucous laughter coming from Charlie confirmed his approval of the stupid stunt. The disapproving glare from the transport lady said otherwise. Knox couldn't get the vehicle in park fast enough. He bolted from the driver's side and grabbed the wheelchair from Henry. "I'll take it from here." Guiding him in the direction of the passenger's side of the car, Knox shushed his uncle who was shouting goodbye to Ol' Man Henry with a thumbs-up high in the air. Knox rolled his eyes and whispered an apology to the transport lady.

She grinned and shrugged before heading toward the hospital entrance. "Good luck with that one," she warned with a wink.

"Really? Was that necessary?" asked Knox once safely inside.

His uncle smirked. "Probably not, but we had fun. I can always count on Henry for a good time."

"No doubt," Knox admitted, shaking his head. This was only the beginning of a long recovery with a stubborn man accustomed to calling the shots.

****

The bumpy ride took a toll on Uncle Charlie's

weakened body. "I don't feel well," he moaned when they finally arrived home.

"Let's get you in the house and straight into the hospital bed. I set it up in the family room." Having him dressed in lounge clothes made it easy to slip him right under the sheets. "Let's ice your hip down." Knox carried an ice pack from the kitchen. "Why don't you rest your eyes for a few minutes while I make you something quick to eat? Almost time for your next dose of pain medication." From his heavy eyelids, Knox realized he only had a short window of time until his uncle was out cold.

"Saltine crackers. In the cupboard top left and grab a ginger ale from the outside refrigerator," Uncle Charlie mumbled.

Knox set the crackers, a soft drink, and pain pill by the bedside. "Let's get a little food in you before you take the pill. I have a feeling you'll be conking out soon." Once the medicine was delivered, he tidied up. "Do you mind if I step out and meet Cate for a quick lunch? Mayor Sam is on his way over for a visit. I'll wait until he arrives before I take off."

Too late for an answer. Uncle Charlie was already fast asleep. Knox removed the ice pack, tucked him in, and ensured the television remote control was within his grasp.

In the kitchen, Knox poured himself a glass of sweet tea. Leaning up against the counter, he texted Cate to see if she wanted to grab a quick bite.

After some time, Sam arrived. "I'm here to relieve you of your duties. How's the patient?" Sam held a newspaper under his arm and a cup of coffee in his hand.

"Out cold. Thanks for coming by. I won't be long."

Trading Henry's old clunker for the golf cart, Knox left for Guest Services. The day was only half over and Knox was already exhausted. He second-guessed his ability to balance his responsibilities to his uncle while actively pursuing a relationship with Cate. He was becoming leery of the whole scavenger hunt game plan, too. Truly, his time would be better spent caring for his uncle than running around the island in search of stamps. Willing to put aside his fears for the time being, he continued on his way fully intent on enjoying the time with Cate.

As per usual, Cate was running late.

Knox took it upon himself to head over to Island Scoop and order takeout for the two of them. The shop served a limited lunchtime menu like an old-fashioned drug store. "Two cheeseburger and fry specials to go. Wrapped separately, please," Knox ordered at the counter. "An extra side of crisp dill pickles for each, too."

The older lady at the register smiled. "You got it, honey. Order number twenty-three." She handed him the receipt.

Knox removed his scavenger hunt passport from his pocket.

"Give it here, sweetie." She stamped it with Island Scoop insignia and handed it back.

"My, um, Cate will need a stamp, too. She's not here yet." He struggled with what to call her…friend, ex, girlfriend.

"Send her on over when she does. I'll take care of it, dear," offered the salt-and-pepper-haired woman.

Knox sighed. One less thing to worry about for

now.

In a flash, lunch was served in two paper sacks. Striding out the door, he bumped into Cate.

"Sorry I'm late. Kelsey received a phone call from corporate and then a newlywed couple arrived to check in for the week. They were hoping for a stress-free stay far away from family," she rambled.

Knox couldn't determine if his hunger or the sound of the word newlywed caused his guard to go up. A lifetime commitment was the last thing he wanted right now. Making a split decision, he handed one of the sacks to Cate. "Sorry," he blurted. "I can't stay for lunch. Uncle Charlie needs me right now."

"What is it?" she cried, her forehead wrinkled. "Is he in pain?"

"Terrible," he fibbed, kicking himself for betraying her.

"Is there anything I can do to help?" she asked.

He wished he could take back what he just said. Rather than clam up, he did the right thing. "I meant to say the pain has been terrible off and on. Mayor Sam is at the house. I'd feel better if I was there."

Something in her face shifted. "Oh, I understand completely. I'll be fine. Please, take your burger and go." She waved him off with a hand.

"Don't forget to have your passport stamped. The nice lady at the counter said she'd take care of it for you."

"Sure thing. I'll head in right away before I forget." Cate lingered.

Feeling the stress to be the person Cate deserved, he relented. "If you don't mind chicken, mashed potatoes, and gelatin, you could join us for supper. Six o'clock?"

"I can't wait," she replied in a soft voice, with the hint of a smile and lips parted.

Knox inched a step forward, eager for her to speak, but only silence filled the space between them.

She studied him for a moment, batting her eyelashes, and then quietly strode away.

He propped his hands on his hips to steady himself, flushed with excitement for what tonight might bring.

****

The gentle breeze wafted the smell of the freshly chargrilled cheeseburger and Old Bay fries Cate was carrying back to her office. Wrapped in red-and-white-checked paper inside the Island Scoop signature sack, the burger and fry combo was a favorite on the island. Cate's persistent hunger pains tempted her to rip the bag open and take a ginormous bite. If she wasn't out in public, there would have been no stopping her. Common sense told her she needed to preserve her image as the new manager of Guest Services. Patience prevailed as she hightailed it back in record time to savor it uninterrupted.

Cate spent the morning with Kelsey in orientation lockdown, as Eliza dubbed it. The topics of the day included payroll and expenses, inventory control, and seasonal rates. All of which were familiar to Cate in some capacity, making the learning curve less steep than it could have been. Kelsey was a stickler for using the company manual as a guide to all decision making. Already Cate witnessed a notable difference in their management styles as she was much more relaxed, though no less dedicated.

With her break almost over, Cate hurried inside

and sat at the front desk. Meals were supposed to be eaten in the back, but not this time. Being alone in the building fueled Cate's wild side. Nibbling on the crisp, salted fries, she leaned back, her mind wandering to Knox. The mixed messages he sent troubled her. Initially all in for date night, the vibe he gave off at the restaurant was more lukewarm than hot.

The same held true today. Cate was super excited to get his text asking her to meet up for a quick lunch. Making it happen on her end was no easy task. With Kelsey fixated on Cate's orientation and Eliza finishing the welcome packages, neither of her co-workers was in a hurry to take a break. Usually Eliza was the one who hinted to switch the sign to *Closed*, but not today. Hearing Kelsey finally give the green light, Cate practically ran them over on her way out the door. Now she questioned if Knox even appreciated her extra effort to make it happen.

Chapter Ten

Cate peered up from her phone to see Eliza cross the threshold with only a few minutes to spare. The empty French fry wrapper and ketchup packets strewn across the counter grabbed her friend's attention.

"A little liberal with the rules, I see." Eliza snatched up a lone remaining fry and popped it in her mouth. "How was Mr. Wonderful?"

"Unpredictable." Cate frowned.

"How so?" Eliza rested her elbows on the counter with her fists under her chin.

"So here's the confusing thing. He invites me to a spontaneous lunch at Island Scoop for a burger and fries, which are delicious, and then ditches me when I get there…" She tossed her trash in the bin.

"Ouch," exclaimed Eliza.

"I know, right? But then as he's leaving, he extends an invitation to join him and his uncle for dinner. Go figure." Cate threw her hands in the air.

"If I were you, I'd eat something beforehand. Odds are you're going home hungry tonight."

"Don't I know it," Cate agreed.

Kelsey bustled through the front door. "Lunch is officially over. I have a quick call to make and then we are moving on to inventory control." She dashed to her office and firmly closed the door.

Kelsey didn't usually take a call in private unless

the office was crowded with guests. Something was up, and Cate was curious as to what.

Eliza trotted over to the front door and flipped the sign to *Open*. "Psst. Ms. Manager-elect. I wanted to give you a heads-up since you're not a big fan of surprises."

"Shoot." Cate piled the registration packets from underneath the counter on the desk. "Let's organize these as we talk."

"A new gallery is opening in Charleston Saturday night. If possible, Will and I were *hoping* to head there after the scavenger hunt announcement tomorrow at five and stay at his aunt and uncle's house on the Battery. Just a couple of nights. The forecast is calling for sunny skies and mild temperatures. Perfect weather to visit the Holy City."

"What?" Cate handed Eliza packets to stack on the countertop.

"Oh, we'll come back early Sunday morning so I can work my usual shift." Eliza climbed onto her stool for a better view.

Cate stopped and stared. "So, you're asking Kelsey for Saturday off?"

Eliza chuckled. "Um, yes or maybe you could ask for me? I can't be here and there at the same time. This gallery has expressed an interest in my work. And, listen to this. Will's uncle has a business connection with the owner, so he offered to make an introduction. Can you believe my luck?" She shrugged and raised her hands.

Slowly inhaling, Cate counted to four and then exhaled. When she decided to take this position, she was well aware that making hard decisions concerning her friendship with Eliza would be part of the job. She just didn't realize it would be happening so soon.

"I promise to make it up. Pinky swear." Eliza wiggled her little finger.

Kelsey swung open her office door. "Cate. I'm ready for you. Inventory Control."

"If you can work it into your conversation with Kelsey, I wouldn't object. You got this, sister," Eliza whispered.

Cate held her tongue and nodded slightly. Her disappointment was hard to conceal, but for the sake of their friendship, she must do just that. Tomorrow was the last day of Cate's training. If Kelsey green lighted Eliza's request, Cate would handle the Saturday morning departures and afternoon arrivals all by herself. The only way that situation would work was if Eliza prepped all the welcome packets ahead of time while tending the front desk on Friday. But even so, Guest Services would be swamped on Saturday.

In all fairness, Cate realized her needs didn't trump Eliza's. Both of them were simply chasing their dreams at the same time. The smooth transition from employee to boss she imagined might just be more problematic than envisioned.

Eliza tugged on Cate's shirt. "Don't forget these." She handed Cate the notebook and Guest Services manual.

The simple gesture made the time-off request a little more palatable. They would always have each other's backs. This slight hiccup might be the first of more to come, but for now, she had to focus on making the best decisions for Guest Services.

The afternoon in Kelsey's office whizzed by as

Cate learned about the importance of keeping a handle on the inventory. Rental properties were often in flux, meaning Cate would need to be on her toes while managing her available properties for rent.

Kelsey offered her views on tracking the inventory in the system and encouraged Cate to tweak it if need be. The pair worked side by side making the best use of their limited time together.

She tucked away what she learned for later. The most notable takeaway was the increased demand for eco-friendly rentals. This island trend was yet another reason she needed to persuade Knox to help the Purdeys market their own natural construction business.

"Do you have any questions?" Kelsey asked when the clock struck five.

"Is there a plan for tomorrow?" Cate inquired solely for the purpose of dropping the bomb about Eliza's request for time off. The rumbling from her stomach matched her uneasiness.

"No agenda for tomorrow, but I do want to speak with you now about personnel. We haven't touched upon the backbone of the organization. I'm afraid we'll need to address it sooner rather than later. You are only as good as the people who surround you. Find employees you can learn from and support them every step of the way. Don't hold them back, and you will reap the rewards of being a mentor. The best advice I can give is to continue to grow, professionally and personally. Life is a continuous lesson in learning. Take it from me. Keep evolving. You'll never regret it." Kelsey picked up her phone and checked the time.

"Speaking of employees, Eliza was hoping to take off Saturday." Cate paused to read Kelsey before continuing.

Her head jerked up. "Arrival and departure day?"

Cate laughed nervously. "Right? Saturday. Busiest day of the week. But, she has a very good reason. A potential step forward in her art career. And from what I've heard you say, we, I mean you, should probably let her go. She does have remaining vacation days to use. I verified it."

Kelsey folded her hands together. "You're a fast learner. That's why I'm putting you in charge. Figure out what works best for you...and Guest Services. I'm confident you'll come to the right decision."

"Thanks, Kelsey." Cate kept her tone as neutral as possible.

"Also, don't forget. You need to find your replacement." She lifted an eyebrow.

"Sure. I can think about it over the weekend. Maybe I can ask around and see if anyone is in need of a job," Cate suggested.

Kelsey stood and began gathering her things. She withdrew a cardboard box from her closet. "I didn't want to spring this upon you earlier for fear you might have panicked. Today's topic was much too important to discuss without being distracted."

Cate could sense this conversation would not end well.

"Today is my last day," she announced. "Corporate mixed up the dates. The paperwork has been processed, and it can't be changed. In normal circumstances, I'd stay and finish out the week without being compensated. However, my mother is ill, which is why I'm choosing to embrace this slip-up and take off for Atlanta a day early. I'm sure you understand. If I was leaving anyone but you in charge, I'd go to bat with corporate and have it reversed. But truly, not necessary. I did take the opportunity to line up several interviews for Saturday morning. I hoped to be here to assist through your first hiring process, but I feel certain you'll find just the right candidate on your own."

"So, what exactly are you saying?" she sputtered with trembling lips and watery eyes. Cate couldn't get the words out fast enough. "Not supposed to happen this way." She rubbed the back of her neck.

"I'm saying congratulations, Cate Ainsworth. You're now officially the new manager of Guest Services." Kelsey continued cleaning out her office. "Quite frankly, you and I both know you didn't really need this orientation. You've been preparing for this day for years. Take this job and run with it, Cate. Make this place your own. You have some big decisions to make. I've full confidence in you, and so does corporate."

Cate's eyes welled with tears. Her dream was coming true, not tied up in a pretty bow as she expected, but she didn't care. The end result was the same, even if the office was falling apart.

For the past three years, Cate reported to Kelsey. Their relationship has been strictly professional, mostly due to their age difference. Funny with it coming to an end, Cate wished for more time to fully take advantage of Kelsey's wisdom and experience. Kelsey's influence on Cate was what she'd come to rely on when faced with challenging decisions. The first of which would be dealing with Eliza's request for time off.

As Kelsey made one final sweep of her office, Cate bit her lip in an effort to stop it from trembling. Saying goodbye had never been easy for Cate, especially with someone she'd probably never see again.

"I think that's everything. If you find anything else that's mine, please send it along. I'll email you my forwarding address." Kelsey smiled warmly at Cate.

A tear trickled down Cate's cheek followed by a few more. The two embraced, with Kelsey rubbing Cate's back for comfort. "Thank you, Kelsey, for having faith in me. I promise not to let you down." Cate fiddled with her earring.

"You're going to do just fine, Cate," she assured her replacement, opening the door to the office.

Cate picked up on her subtle cue and proceeded back to the front counter before her emotional state worsened. Her boss was short on time and not equipped for a long goodbye.

Eliza shot her a what-the-heck look and then directed her attention to Kelsey.

"Best of luck with your pursuit of art. I enjoyed working with you." Kelsey extended a hand.

"Cate," said Kelsey mid-step. "Tomorrow is payroll. Don't forget to submit it before nine." She continued toward the front door.

"Will do!" Cate snapped back, adding the task to her long list of mental notes.

"What did she say?" Eliza didn't even wait until the door closed before bombarding Cate with questions.

She held up a hand. "Please wait. Give me a second, and I'll explain." Cate darted to the front door and flipped the sign back to *Closed*. "Kelsey is catching a plane to Atlanta tonight. Corporate mixed up her exit date and—"

"How can that be?" Eliza scrunched her nose and

forehead.

A loud bang at the door scared Cate half to death. Pivoting, she noticed the delivery man standing there and holding a small package. Quickly, she thrust open the glass door and grabbed it.

The friendly guy waved goodbye and left.

Curious about its contents, she went over to the desk and rummaged in the drawer for a pair of scissors. "So, as I was saying, today was Kelsey's last day." Cate opened the box and extracted a stack of glossy, blue-and-white business cards emblazoned with her name followed by the word...*manager*. She grabbed her phone and snapped a pic. Hitting send, she couldn't resist a little giggle. Almost immediately, she received a reply. A thumbs-up emoji from Grammy put everything into perspective. She needed to step up and be the boss.

She put the cards aside. "So, here's the deal. Earlier in the week, Kelsey set up appointments for Saturday to interview candidates to replace me. Initially, she planned to guide me through the process, but now everything is on me. I hate to do it, Eliza, but I can't give you the day off. I'm going to need you to handle the Saturday departures while I meet with potential hires. And, since tomorrow is my first day on my own and I have to get payroll done, I'm depending on you to get the welcome packets together ahead of time."

"But..."

"Please let me finish." Eliza's blatant grimace did little to deter Cate. "What I am able to do is let you leave at four o'clock on Saturday so at least you can make it to Charleston in time for the gallery opening. By that time, most of the arrivals will have checked in.

The best I can do in these circumstances." Cate chewed on her lip, waiting for Eliza to react to the news.

"All right." She exhaled noisily through pursed lips. "I'm not going to lie. I'm disappointed, but I guess that's fair. I better go tell Will. Last we talked, he was packing the car. Anything else I need to know before we lock up for the night?" She pointed toward the clock on the wall.

Cate glanced over. Fewer than fifteen minutes to pick up a pie and make it to Uncle Charlie's. "No, I think we're good. Listen, I wouldn't be in this position if it weren't for your support. I love you, Eliza."

Eliza hugged her friend. "I love you, too. Now get out of here. You're going to be late, again."

Cate fluttered her lashes and flashed a grin in anticipation.

****

While preparing for Cate's arrival, Knox kept his eye on his uncle's kitchen clock. He parked his uncle in the recliner and handed him the remote control. Satisfied his uncle was taken care of for the time being, Knox focused his energy on putting dinner together. Preparing the meal was a welcome distraction from his caregiver duties. Since he took time to pre-cook the dinner, a quick zap in the microwave was all he needed to do.

"I'm guessing the date fared much better than what you're letting on, son. Fancy linens and flowers equal love, if you ask me. Go ahead and change your clothes, she should be here any minute. The clock says five of six."

Knox placed the butter dish on the table. "I've got at least fifteen more minutes. I told her six, but I'm not serving dinner until six-fifteen. And, c'mon, we're talking Cate here. Odds are she'll be late."

Charlie laughed. "I spent most of my life waiting for your aunt. Might as well get used to it."

Knox was encouraged by his uncle's better frame of mind. The day had been a roller coaster ride of emotions for both of them. The new normal would take some time to get used to. And, time was something they had plenty of right now. Cate would be a good buffer between them. Her bubbly personality brightened any conversation. Ending the day on a positive note would serve them well for the long days ahead.

The sound of the doorbell ringing caught him by surprise.

"Six o'clock," said Knox incredulously.

"On the dot," Uncle Charlie punctuated.

Knox wiped his hands on the kitchen towel. Glancing at the table, he double-checked that all the utensils were in place and, with a lighter in hand, lit the lemon-scented candle in the middle of the table. For an impromptu dinner, Knox was stopping at nothing to win over Cate.

"Are you going to answer the door? She's on time for once. Let her revel in the small victory," shouted Uncle Charlie from his recliner.

"Yes, sir." Knox checked his breath in his palm, and then swung open the front door. Knox stepped aside while Cate made herself at home in her typical fashion.

"Hello," her voice filled the small space. Still in work attire, she gave Knox a quick peck on the cheek and handed him a pie box. "Thanks for inviting me over. Where's the rock star patient?" She waltzed in with a blue gift bag in tow. "For someone newly released from the hospital, you appear healthy as a horse." Cate handed Uncle Charlie the gift. "Something to keep you busy."

The way Uncle Charlie's face brightened confirmed what Knox knew all along. The reason he returned to Gull Island was standing right in the middle of the living room. His heart swelled with happiness.

"Catie-bird, come sit and tell me all about your new job. Knox started to fill me in before you showed up, on time, I might add."

She collapsed on the couch. "You first," she insisted. "How are you feeling?"

Knox excused himself to the kitchen to put the finishing touches on dinner, allowing Uncle Charlie to take advantage of having Cate's ear. His uncle insisted on retelling his hospital woes from the very beginning, not realizing Cate had been kept informed by Knox from the start. When he got to the part about his persistent nurse, Knox stepped in.

"Dinner is served," he announced in a snooty accent.

Cate chuckled, outwardly pleased by his silliness.

Like a good caregiver, he swooped to his uncle's aid by helping him out of the chair. Taking one step at a time, they made it to the table.

Knox sneaked a peek at Cate while adjusting Charlie in his chair, hoping for some sort of reaction to the yellow-themed table he'd set. He observed her admiring the pretty napkins and even caught her inching forward to smell the burning candle. Once seated, he began passing dishes of food.

"The food smells delicious. My compliments to the

chef." She clapped her hands.

"I fixed some good ol' comfort food for Uncle Charlie's first night home, and for you." There, he said it. No more secrets.

"And you did. Bravo." Cate raised her glass filled with sweet tea for a toast.

The men followed along in the fun.

"How did the training go today?" Knox swiftly changed the topic.

With a mouthful of food, she held up her pointer finger to give herself a moment to swallow. "Anything but ordinary."

"I imagine you've covered the main topics by now. Tomorrow, I'm sure Kelsey will focus more on tying up loose ends. The minutiae will wait until Monday," Knox said.

Placing the fork and knife on her plate, she shook her head from side to side. "Oh, training is over. Today was Kelsey's last day." She smacked her lips.

"What? Wait, you said her last day was Friday." Knox peered over at Uncle Charlie who was just as surprised by the news as he was. Neither had any opportunity to offer his two cents because Cate hijacked the conversation, barely stopping long enough to catch her breath. Midway through, she handed each her new business card.

"So, to recap, forget about the marketing strategy or anything else I might have told you. My number one priority is to hire my replacement. Kelsey lined up three candidates for Saturday, the busiest day of the week. Tonight, when I get home, I need to search the web on how to interview someone for a job." Cate finally paused to breathe.

"That's one way to do it. I'm liking your take-charge approach," Knox complimented her. From the corner of his eye, he caught Uncle Charlie trying to hide a yawn. The long day was catching up to him.

"Whatta ya say we slice up the peach pie you brought?" Uncle Charlie interjected, rubbing his eyes.

Cate laughed. "Did I mention peach?"

"The box says Island Scoop. What else would it be?" He gestured with his hands in the air.

"My uncle does have a point," agreed Knox.

"With or without ice cream?" asked Cate.

"Ice cream, please," his uncle demanded.

Cate scooted her chair back from the table, gathering plates. "Why don't I help you in the kitchen?"

"Good idea, Catie-bird. Make sure he doesn't shortchange me on the ice cream."

Shaking his head, Knox made his way to the kitchen. "Just stack the dishes in the sink. I'll load the dishwasher after you leave." He grabbed the pie box and set it on the island in the middle of the kitchen. In the freezer, he found the ice cream hidden in the back.

"Nonsense, I'll rinse and load while you get dessert ready." Cate got busy at the sink.

Knox drew out a cake knife from the drawer. "If you think it would be helpful, I'd be happy to offer some tips for interviewing potential new hires." Cate didn't say anything at first, making Knox think he'd overstepped. He pretended to be concentrating on slicing the pie, making sure each piece was equal.

"I appreciate the offer," she said. A muscle in her jaw twitched. "Let me take a peek at the notes Kelsey left me before I drag you into this. I realize how busy you are right now."

"Of course," he quickly added. "If we hurry, I bet we can earn another stamp by catching the sunset. That is if you think you have enough time. I don't want to cut into your research time."

Cate put down the kitchen towel in her hand. "What about the pie and Uncle Charlie?"

Knox inched closer, resting an elbow on the kitchen sink. "Pie first. As for Uncle Charlie, he can't get rid of me fast enough." Cate paused long enough to make him think she was truly weighing her options.

"What are we waiting for?" she replied.

Knox asked himself the very same question. Perhaps tonight, he'd finally get the answer.

****

The scenic drive to the inlet captured Cate's attention. Admiring the island's natural beauty never got old.

"Before we get sidetracked, let's talk about what questions to ask potential new hires," Knox suggested.

"I think questions like why'd you apply, what experience do you bring to guest services, and how well-versed are you on island life would be a good start," Cate spouted off, fully prepared from her homework.

"That's very clever of you to include the island in your discussion. Three solid questions. I like it. What else?" He prodded her.

"What's your proudest achievement outside of work?" She tilted her head to the side.

Knox's body stiffened. "Are you asking me, or is this one of your questions?"

Cate swatted at a fly inside the windshield. "Both," she said, anxious to hear his reply.

Knox veered into the opposite lane to get around a pokey golf cart.

The pesky fly took advantage of the breeze and flew to safety.

"First, you have a valid question to ask the interviewee. It'll enable you to see another side of the person. Get to know them better without appearing too nosy."

"And second?" She wasn't letting him off easy.

After rolling up to the stop sign, Knox halted abruptly. "My proudest achievement was falling in love with you." He glanced both ways and continued driving.

His words were impactful, truly what she wanted to hear from his lips. Yet, she needed a moment to let them sink in. She couldn't accept them at face value. "If that is true, then why did you leave?" she said, barely above a whisper.

Knox licked his lips.

Cate noted him biding his time, hoping he'd deliver the answer she needed to hear.

"I was a coward. Afraid of the unknown. So I ran away, fooling myself by saying I was running toward adventure and excitement. If I could do it all over again, the outcome would be very different," he admitted.

Cate swallowed hard. She deserved an explanation. Heck, she demanded an explanation.

"I didn't expect us to have this conversation in my truck tonight, but I guess now is as good a time as any. I owe you an apology for screwing up. I was selfish, not thinking straight. I want to make it up to you. I probably don't deserve it, but I hope you can forgive me, and maybe even be open to giving me a second

149

chance." His gaze darted in her direction and then back on the road. Drumming his fingertips on the steering wheel, he probably waited for her to speak.

Now, her chance had come.

Chapter Eleven

"You left for college without giving me so much as a reason why we were no longer a couple. You cut me off completely. Even blocked me on your phone. What was I to think?" Cate willed her hands to stop shaking. "Our last conversation at the pier played over and over in my head. I was searching for some clue as to why you slipped away. I'd always been there for you, especially when times were not so great between you and your parents. Remember when you fought with your dad the summer of freshman year? I let you hide out in the boathouse—for three whole days. I even snuck your meals. I'll never forget the relief on your dad's face when I escorted you back home. He had been worried sick." She crossed her arms over her chest.

"I'm sorry, Cate," he interjected.

"I know you are, Knox. I'm not trying to make you feel bad. I just want you to understand where I'm coming from. I trusted you with my heart, my secrets, and my soul," she professed, her tone even. "Then one day, I woke up to lessening pain and a mended heart. I realized you did me a favor. I figured out who I am and what makes me happy. Life returned to normal, a new normal without Knox Price. And now, you're here—asking me for another chance. I wish I could say I have no room for you in my life anymore, but that would be a lie," she admitted.

"Really?" He gripped the steering wheel with both hands.

"Really, but I'm going to have to learn to trust you, and trust builds over time. We all make mistakes." Cate tugged at her ear.

Knox drove toward the inlet in silence. Arriving at their destination, he threw the truck in Park. "This is not a mistake."

Cate waited as he leaned as far as his seatbelt would stretch and gently kissed her on the lips. She never expected to be sitting in his truck with their lips touching and her heart melting. She could not deny the attraction. If she wanted to proceed, the first step would have to be forgiveness.

"I had to leave. I needed to see what the world had to offer." A muscle in his jaw twitched.

"And now," Cate whispered. "Are you willing to stick around for good, or is this another stop along the way?"

"I want to see where this goes, Cate. I realize Uncle Charlie's surgery wasn't the only reason for me coming back home. I had to see you. I had to make it right." He brushed the hair away from her eyes.

"Look at this place." She pointed to the inlet. "Why would you ever want to leave?" Her question was more of a statement. She wasn't seeking an answer. For so long, she dreamed of this very moment—wished for a chance to start all over again. The time had come to open her heart. "The sunlight is fading. If we don't hurry, we'll miss the sunset." Cate was ready to dash ahead.

Knox followed her lead. "C'mon. Let's go."

Cate was giddy when Knox reached for her hand outside the truck and led her toward the crowds gathered by the rocks. The two jockeyed for position among the others to capture the best angle of the setting sun. Cate held her phone out in front of them and took a bunch of pics. The first two were at an odd angle. All they could see was a blurred close-up of their faces along with red, orange, and yellow streaks in the sky. The sun was nowhere to be found. "Remind me again. To earn the stamp, we must capture the setting sun with us in the picture frame, correct?"

"That's what I think," his voice lingered. The Friday deadline was looming, and even Knox strained to make it to the finish line.

She passed him the phone for a look-see.

"This one isn't too bad." He pointed to the photo. "Here's the sun and part of my forehead and the top of your head." Their size difference wasn't helping with getting the right shot.

Cate perceived something in his composure shift. Maybe the sight of his crooked smile or the release of tension from his brow. Their renewed familiarity gave her a profound awareness of hope. This was their second act. "Maybe it'd be better if you take the photo," she suggested. "Your arms are longer than mine."

"Good idea." He reached out for her phone. "Let's think this through. We need to angle the pic from low to high, which means…"

"I need to be in front of you," she finished his sentence.

"Exactly." He smiled. "Which rocks would work best?"

They both searched about, but other contestants

were occupying the rocks close by.

"If you don't mind getting sandy, we could sit together on the jetty," Cate suggested.

"Why didn't I think of that?" he asked. "C'mon."

The rocks lined the inlet on both sides, enabling boats to pass easily on their way out to sea. Cate and Knox traipsed about twenty-five yards, far enough away from the crowd to capture their shot without others intruding on their space. The sun dipped lower, almost disappearing on the horizon. If they didn't hurry, they would miss it.

He sat, folding his legs and resting his hands on his knees.

"Where do you want me?" Cate asked, realizing time was of the essence.

"Next to me." He patted the rock to his right.

She copied how he was sitting with her legs folded and waited for him to start snapping away.

Inching closer, he wrapped one arm around her and used the other to hold the phone, stretched out far in front of them.

Cate leaned back against his chest, nestling her head in the crook of his neck.

"Smile," he said.

How could she not? The warmth of his toned arms quickened her pulse.

Twenty or so pictures later, Knox captured the perfect shot. He handed the phone back to Cate. "All we need now is to post it on social media with the hashtag #GISunset."

"Leave that to me." Using the contest's hashtag, she scrolled through the pictures curious as to what the others posted.

"I hate to cut this short, but I better get back to Uncle Charlie." His lips dipped into a frown.

"I don't hear any sirens, so I take that as a good sign that he hasn't burned down the house," she joked, brushing the sand off her clothes. Satisfied with their photo, she hurriedly shared it on social media.

"Don't tempt fate," Knox warned.

Cate stepped next to him, waiting to see if he would hold her hand on the way back to the truck. When she glanced in his direction, she noticed him quickly sending off a text.

"Uncle Charlie. For the man who claimed to be totally against any form of modern technology, he sure has embraced the use of his new cell phone. He was practically kicking and screaming when I told him he was getting one. Now, he won't stop texting me." He gestured to the long stream of messages.

"I could say the same thing about Grammy. She sends me more texts than my mother. Go figure."

As they climbed into the truck, the conversation circled back to Cate's job interviews scheduled for Saturday. Cate liked Knox's suggestion of jotting down a wish list of qualities she was seeking in a candidate before talking to the potential hires. An impromptu role play by Knox mimicking a potential scenario gave Cate some useful ideas.

When they neared the beach cottage, he eased off the gas pedal. "That about covers everything. My best advice is to be thorough. Let the interviewee do most of the talking. Listen to what the person is saying and don't be afraid to put them on the spot."

"Got it," she replied, with her signature sing-songy voice. Being prepared was the best way to approach it, and after talking with him, Cate's confidence in handling it on her own soared.

"Only one thing left to discuss before I drop you off." He stopped short to let a wayward deer continue across the road.

Cate's mind started spinning. Hadn't they hashed out everything that needed to be discussed? What more could he possibly want to talk about? "Oh," she answered, trying to sound comfortable with his request.

"With the change in your work calendar, I have no problem taking Jackson to the preliminaries on Saturday morning by myself. He seems to think we'll be done by two, which puts us back on Gull Island no later than four. I'm sure I can strong-arm Ol' Man Henry into coming back to the house to keep an eye on Uncle Charlie, especially if peach pie with vanilla ice cream is involved," Knox offered.

All at once, the tipping point of teetering between her personal and professional life came to a head. Cate's resilience was being tested in ways she never could have imagined. If she was serious about taking her career and personal life to the next level, the first step would have to be delegating some of her responsibilities to capable hands, like Knox. "Thank you."

Knox hesitated. "So, you're okay with me taking him?"

Her smile brightened. "I'm more than okay." Standing on the gravel driveway at the beach house with the full moon shining down, Cate waved goodbye to Knox. She remained there until the taillights on his truck faded away.

Tonight marked a turning point in something she

never imagined. She and Knox were picking up where they left off. This time, they were two entirely different people. What made their renewed relationship special was a mutual respect for the life they each experienced in the intervening years, making a proverbial clean slate for both.

Jackson's jeep was parked under the carport.

Practice must have ended early or maybe he was too tired to hang out with his friends. Either way, Cate was happy for the company. She tested the door handle—unlocked per usual. Quite normal in a small town like Gull Island. Tossing her sandy flip-flops by the door, she took the steps two at a time to burn off some energy. When she arrived at the top, she was drawn to the shimmering moonlight dancing on the horizon.

"There you are. How was your date?"

Her quiet moment of calm didn't last long. Cate peeked into the kitchen, finding her brother sitting atop the island with an overstuffed sandwich in hand. "Perfect." She eyed the freezer and took out a pint of vanilla ice cream. Opening the kitchen drawer, she helped herself to a spoon.

"Good. Less awkwardness for the car ride on Saturday." He bit into his homemade sandwich.

Cate popped open the carton and dug out a sizable scoop of frozen deliciousness. "Speaking of Saturday. I'm going to be a no-show. You and Knox will be on your own."

Jackson squinted. "After all that work trying to convince him the idea was his. Why the change in plans?"

"You're not going to believe this. Let me start at

the beginning." Cate filled her brother in concerning Kelsey's quick exit and the need for Cate's crash course in management. By the time she reached the part about the scheduled new hire interviews, she spotted Jackson yawning. "So, you're all caught up." She tossed the spoon in the sink. "I really do apologize for not being able to take you, but you're in capable hands." Placing the remainder of the ice cream in the freezer, she flipped the kitchen light switch and headed to the cozy chair.

Not much later, Jackson shuffled toward his room. "Good night, sis. I'm proud of you. You're going to make an awesome Guest Services Chief of Staff." His deep yawn signaled the end of the busy day.

"Guest Services Manager, not Chief of Staff, but thanks. I appreciate your vote of confidence." Cate lifted a hand in the air and high-fived her brother.

Her brother's words of encouragement made her feel warm and fuzzy. Before Cate dozed off, she wanted to update her vision board. She didn't know how long it would take, so she removed her makeup and changed into shortie pajamas. With yellow slippers on her feet, she was ready to redirect her jitters into something more productive.

Cate propped up her latest board on the kitchen table, using two large cookbooks to make it stand upright. Lugging her materials out from under her bed, she headed to the kitchen to get to work. Twice a day, in the morning and before bed, she made sure to catch a glimpse of the board to remind herself of the goals she set. Her mind and heart were working overtime tonight, meaning she had plenty to add.

First item she cut out from a magazine was a clock.

As a manager, punctuality was absolutely necessary. If she couldn't be on time, why should her employees? Fiddling around with the vision board made her think less about Knox and more about what she'd have to accomplish at the office during the next couple of days. Leafing through a news magazine, she searched for a picture with special meaning to add to the board. "Delegate" was a word that stood out as an important one to include. Letter by letter, she spelled out the word by pasting it at the top of the board. The last thing she did before putting away all the art supplies was cut out a simple red rose. Taking a step back, she paused to take it all in. Her board was shaping up to be a bold reminder of what mattered most.

Climbing into bed, she could feel the butterflies in her tummy fluttering. Tomorrow would be her first day on the job as manager. Forget counting sheep. The only way to fall asleep tonight was to listen to the sound of the waves hitting the shore.

****

The first alarm clock in Cate's bedroom sounded at seven in the morning. The second chimed at seven-thirty. Before the third rang, Cate opened her eyes. She was greeted by Jackson, hanging from the doorframe doing pull-ups.

"You're finally awake," his raspy voice greeted.

"And I didn't even need the third alarm. I woke up on my own. Now that's progress," she announced proudly.

"Thanks to you, I woke up at seven, seven-thirty, and now, nearly eight o'clock. I don't have to be at work until three. Could have used a few extra hours of sleep, but seeing as I'm wide awake and today is your special day, I'm going to make you breakfast. You've got fifteen minutes. Get moving," he ordered.

Throwing the lavender-scented covers aside, Cate darted to the bathroom. While the warmth of the water cascaded down her back, she reviewed what she would wear from head to toe. Juggling too many ideas and responsibilities, she neglected to lay out her clothes the night before. Unlike the front desk positions, she was free to choose her outfit, as long as it fit within the company's business casual guidelines. She'd also have to wear a gold tag sporting her full name and a new title, Guest Services Manager, but that had yet to arrive. So today's outfit would need to be a bit extra.

With less time than anticipated, Cate unplugged her phone from the charger. Sending off a quick text to Knox, she asked if he wouldn't mind swinging by Guest Services to drop off the reservation book to save on time.

Almost immediately, he responded with a stream of emojis including a thumbs-up and happy face.

Clearly, Uncle Charlie was filling in on his behalf. Cate crossed her fingers that he'd remember to tell Knox. In the closet, she withdrew a yellow-and-white sheath dress, similar to what Kelsey commonly wore to work. She slipped it over her head and added some simple gold jewelry. Her hair was not washed, on purpose. Second-day hair was best for wearing in a not-so-messy bun. A light dusting of makeup and lipstick was all she needed. Standing in front of the full-length mirror, she hardly recognized the person staring back. "Shoes, I forgot shoes," she crowed, glancing at her feet. Not prone to wearing heels, she opted for a pair of nude platform sandals.

"Wow. You're official now." Her brother gave her the once-over. "Come eat."

Cate's appetite matched the feast centered on her place at the table. A cup of coffee accompanied the veggie egg white omelet waiting to be eaten. She wasted no time clearing her plate and emptying her mug of joe. As she got ready to leave, Jackson, every bit her supportive little brother, gave his version of a pep talk.

"Be smart. Be kind. Go get 'em!"

"Ra, ra, ra," she chanted, brushing aside the gesture. Deep down, she felt thankful for his good intentions. Cate left the house and headed over to work in the golf cart. A quick glance at her watch confirmed the time shy of eight-thirty. If she hurried, she'd arrive with plenty of time to spare. No need for Cate to use her set of managerial keys upon arrival.

Eliza was already at the Guest Services desk, working hard on the welcome packages.

The two exchanged a quick hug.

"Nice outfit," called Eliza.

Cate rounded the counter toward the office. The anticipation swelled in Cate's chest as she crossed the threshold of Kelsey's office, now hers. She was touched by the company's offer to redecorate it to her liking. The budget was adequate, allowing her to make some simple changes like wall colors and drapes to make it her own. As Cate stared at the pink walls, she reaffirmed that the surrounding aesthetics could definitely use some restyling.

A familiar voice drew Cate to the front desk.

"Good morning, Guest Service Manager." Will saluted her with lots of fanfare.

"I apologize for cutting your and Eliza's trip to Charleston short." Cate gushed her gratitude to Will.

"Not necessary," Will protested. "If I was in your shoes, I would have done the same thing."

Eliza lifted welcome packets off the floor and added them to one of the stacks. "Now would be the perfect time to tell us about your date with Knox."

The friends weren't shy about discussing their personal lives in front of Will. They knew each other too well to hold back. "Everything I hoped for and more, if that's even possible. You'll be happy to know we took a pic of the sunset and tweeted it out, as requested per the contest. We only have one stamp left to get, the nature center."

"You saved the best for last, I see," said Will. "Be sure to say hello to Artie, the baby alligator. He's my personal favorite."

The front door opened, and in strode Knox with the reservation book in hand.

Dressed in shorts and an island T-shirt, Cate might have easily mistaken him for a local.

"Speak of the devil," teased Eliza. "We were just talking about you."

"It better be something good or else I'm keeping this," he kidded.

"Thank you for going out of your way to deliver it," Cate spoke up.

Knox handed it over. "Not a problem. Actually, Bait & Switch was low on change, so I'm headed to the bank next."

"To be honest, I was a little worried you wouldn't get the text," she confessed.

He laughed. "I'm trying to find things to keep

Uncle Charlie occupied. So far, he's taken a liking to being my personal assistant. Next step is to get him to use letters instead of just emojis."

They all laughed.

"Why don't we all meet at the pavilion at five for the big announcement?" Will suggested.

"Let's do it," Knox chimed in.

The others agreed.

Will kissed Eliza goodbye. "I'm heading to the hardware store. See y'all later."

"I'm leaving too," Knox added. "Cate, do you have time for a quick lunch at the nature center? We could grab a bite to eat while getting our final stamp for the contest." He wiggled his brows.

"Sounds good," she said. "Meet you at noon. I promise to text you if I'm running late. I've a feeling today will be busy."

As if on cue, the front door opened just then and a handful of people with completed passports swarmed inside. All of the local businesses were drop-off locations for completed passports.

Eliza stepped up and collected them. Once they left, she deposited the batch into a big box with an opening on top. The passports they collected would eventually be combined with the other stores' collected entries and placed in the drawing.

While Eliza tended to the front desk, Cate busied herself in her new office. With Eliza going out of town, Cate needed to use her time wisely to prepare for the interviews. On the white lacquered desk, she found the notes Kelsey left her along with the three resumes belonging to the interviewees. Time to start reading. Tomorrow would be a long day.

****

On his way to the bank, Knox couldn't stop thinking about Cate, beautifully dressed in her manager attire. He almost said so, but chickened out since he was leery of speaking up in front of Will and Eliza. Ridiculous as that might seem, he was determined to keep his relationship with Cate under wraps for now. He wasn't ready to go public quite yet.

The line at the drive-thru was four cars deep, prompting Knox to park and go inside. To avoid getting caught up in a long-winded conversation with one of Uncle Charlie's cronies, he kept his head down and avoided eye contact while waiting his turn. He noticed only two teller lines were open, opting for the shorter of the two. When the teller finished with the customer in front of him, she posted a *Closed* sign. Knox had a knack for picking the wrong line no matter where he was.

"Knox," squealed a high-pitched voice. "I can't believe my luck." Adeline practically jumped over the counter to greet him. "Where are my manners? How may I help you?"

He removed the green zippered bank bag underneath his arm and placed it on the counter. "Bait & Switch is low on change. Would you mind breaking these bills into ones, fives, and tens?"

She unzipped the bag. "My pleasure." She counted the money and entered the total into the computer. "Beautiful day."

"Mm-hmm," he replied, trying to keep the conversation low-key.

The drawer opened, and she began making stacks of bills. Once she was done counting, she placed them neatly into the green bag. "Psst. Come closer, please." She handed it back.

Knox reluctantly stepped in her direction.

"I applied for the open position at Guest Services. Tomorrow morning, I have an interview with the manager, Kelsey Durbin. Since you're back with Cate, do you think you could ask her to put in a good word for me? I've wanted a job there in like forever."

"But what about your job here at the bank?" he blurted. "So much for keeping my relationship with Cate on the down low," he muttered.

"Between you and me, I'm not very good with numbers," she confessed.

"Oh, really." Knox made a mental note to count his change. The woman behind him in line coughed, clearly bothered by how long he was taking to complete his transaction. Knox took the hint. "Kelsey is no longer working there. Your interview will be with the new manager." He debated whether he should be more forthcoming.

Adeline let out a slow, audible breath, slouching her willowy shoulders and dropping her head.

Knox fiddled with the loose thread from his shirt, ignoring her desperate plea for help.

Chapter Twelve

"Cate is the new manager. If you'd like, I'd be happy to put in a good word for you," Knox offered. The squeal pierced his eardrum. He shot a glance behind him at the grumbling customers waiting in the teller line at the bank.

"Oh, thank you. I appreciate it. Would you like a lollipop? Take two," she insisted.

Grabbing two lime lollipops, he left as fast as his long legs would take him. First thing he did when he sat in the golf cart was count the money. Even if he'd been shortchanged, he wouldn't dare go back. Lesson learned. The drive-thru was the easier way to bank. With no time left to pick up Uncle Charlie's cobbler, he'd have to make do with with the sweets from friends and neighbors.

After checking off everything on Uncle Charlie's to-do list with a quick stop at the store, he returned home. From a few houses away, he spotted Will's truck in the driveway. Knox picked up speed. The window of opportunity to meet Cate was getting smaller by the minute. He couldn't ask Will to leave simply because he scheduled a date with Cate, could he?

Inside the house, laughter sounded from the family room.

He could hear Will and his uncle talking to someone on a video chat. When he neared the couch, he caught a glimpse of his mom on the screen, causing her to pause mid-sentence.

"Is that my favorite son?" Dad's voice bellowed in the background. "Hello, Knox."

"Hey, Mom and Dad." Since his parents had somewhere to be, Knox wasn't forced to make small talk for too long. Once he hung up, he turned toward Will. "A quick stop on your way somewhere else?"

"Checking in on your uncle on my way to the worksite now that he's up for visitors," Will clarified.

Uncle Charlie gave Knox the spiel on what he accomplished since he left. "My therapist said I did much better today. She even suggested some simple exercises I can do during the ballgame."

At Knox's urging, his uncle agreed to stop resisting her advice and get with the program. It sounded like he had taken it to heart.

"A neighbor dropped off some lunch," Uncle Charlie announced. "Probably still warm if you feel like checking."

"I'm taking that as a hint that you're ready to eat." Knox let out a laugh on his way to the kitchen. He set the meal on a TV dinner tray and delivered it to his uncle with a glass of sweet tea. Grabbing the remote, he selected his uncle's favorite news channel as his lunchtime entertainment. "Mayor Sam will be by soon," Knox explained, leaving him the freedom to head out to meet Cate. With a jerk of his head, Knox signaled to Will to get moving.

"Enjoy your lunch. I'm glad you're feeling better." Will playfully squeezed his shoulder.

Charlie waved goodbye, already engrossed in the local news.

"You're all set. Stay seated until Sam gets here. I won't be too long," Knox shouted as he and Will scooted out the back door.

"I hear you and Cate are a couple again. That sure happened fast."

"More or less." He gave Will little to chew on.

"Does Cate realize you're a flight risk?" Will nibbled at a fingernail.

"You make it sound as if I am on trial." Knox leaned against Will's truck.

"Your words, not mine." Will folded his arms across his chest.

Knox kept quiet, curious as to where this conversation was heading.

"I just don't want to see Cate hurt again. That's all. It took a long time for her to let go of the past. Now you're here. You're back together."

"And, your point is?" The thick layer of tension weighed heavy on Knox.

"I'm not going to lie. Cate's not the only one waiting to see if you take off again. Like I said before, Purdey & Son would be very appreciative of your help while you are here. If you decide down the road you're staying, we could talk about making it more permanent. In your hands, friend." He let his arms drop to his side.

Knox glanced at his phone—almost noon. If he didn't leave now, he'd be late for lunch.

"Well, let me let you go. Think about it. We all want you to stay, Knox. If that's what you want to do." He tilted his head to one side.

"I appreciate you stopping by to see Uncle Charlie." Knox kept it simple.

"I know you do," replied Will. "Better get going.

You don't want to keep Cate waiting too long." He climbed into the driver's side.

Knox watched his childhood friend head in the opposite direction. *Please let me make the right decision.*

****

The nature center located on the south side of the island had undergone an extensive renovation, taking close to eighteen months from start to finish. Cate intended to stop by and check it out, but she never got around to it for one reason or another. Meeting Knox here enabled her to explore a tourist destination Guest Services often recommended. Being knowledgeable about one of the island's newest treasures was a top priority as the new manager.

The project was completed just in time for the summertime rush. Cate was struck by the array of live displays, as well as the informational exhibits about plants and animals native to the area. As an added perk, a cafe was added, serving snacks and light fare. Tables were immersed in the natural habitat to give it more of an island feel.

She was surprised Knox was running late. Like her brother, he prided himself on being habitually early. Chalking it up to something having to do with his uncle, she helped herself to a menu and planted herself at a long wooden table in the shade to wait.

Perusing the menu, she noticed locally sourced items, a commonality among shops and small businesses here on the island. She had a hard time deciding between the seafood salad or fish and chips. The snug fit of her dress made her lean toward the salad option. Then again, she had a hankering for an oyster po'boy, always a favorite here on the island.

The reptile demonstration not far from where she was seated caught her attention. The slithery snake wrapped around the handler's arm sent chills down her spine. A low hissing sound in her ear sent Cate jumping out of her seat and right into the arms of Knox.

"I gotcha," he shouted, a little too loud.

She squeezed him tight for a brief moment, then playfully beat her fists on his chest in protest. "Knox Price. You scared me half to death."

"Shh," an older woman seated nearby scolded the couple, sending them both into a fit of giggles.

Playing it cool, Cate released herself from his arms and sat, with Knox following her lead. She pretended to be engrossed in all things reptile when truly she couldn't help herself from stealing glances at him.

"Sorry I'm late," he whispered.

"If I had a dime for every time I was late, I'd be rich by now," she blurted.

They both laughed at her self-realization, funny but true.

"Was it your uncle?" At the conclusion of the demonstration, she clapped along with the crowd.

He shook his head.

"Care to expand?" she pried.

He toyed with a paper straw left on the table. "Will stopped by to see my uncle. Slowed me down. Have you decided on lunch?"

Recognizing his change of subject, Cate let it slide...for now. She had a funny feeling something happened between the two friends. "I'm leaning toward the oyster po'boy and sweet tea, the nectar of the gods. And you?"

He let out a laugh. "You and your sweet tea. I think it runs through your veins."

"Maybe," she teased.

"I'll go with the shrimp po'boy. Since we are short on time, I'll go place the order. Be right back."

Cate took a deep breath. Her mind was filled with more details than she could possibly remember. Grabbing her new company-issued planner, she jotted down notes about things to do at work. She periodically checked on Knox, waiting at the counter for the order.

"Lunch has arrived," Knox announced from afar, holding two baskets overflowing with fried seafood.

She popped her planner back into her purse. His arm brushed hers, placing her lunch order and his on the table.

"Extra napkins for you and extra ketchup for me."

Even though the oysters weren't freshly harvested—it was June, after all—Cate savored the flavor of the crispy coating when she bit into her sandwich. Fresh oysters were only available from September through April.

Knox devoured his sandwich, barely coming up for breath between each bite.

She skipped small talk in favor of eating, due to a self-imposed time crunch.

"This hit the spot. How's yours?" Knox popped a hush puppy into his mouth.

"Absolutely delicious. Thanks for inviting me here. I wish I could stick around longer, but I need to get back." She rubbed her hands together. "I haven't even reviewed the resumes yet. Prepping for the interviews is on my agenda for this afternoon. I have to check the candidates' backgrounds and social media accounts for any red flags. Learned that from the notes Kelsey left for me. At least I have somewhere to start. The rest is a bit murky, but I'll plow through it." She offered a half-smile.

"Actually, I wanted to talk with you about that." He sipped his coke, washing down his last bite.

Cate's planner was on the table, ready for her to take notes. Figuring he was about to offer some noteworthy advice, she grabbed her favorite black pen. "I'll take any advice I can get on the subject. Think you can give me a crash course in under fifteen minutes?"

Knox wiped his mouth. "You don't need a crash course. You're a natural at this. What I wanted to tell you is that Adeline, Mayor Sam's daughter, is one of your applicants."

"Really? Why didn't you tell me this morning when you dropped off the book?"

He slid the basket aside and set his forearms on the table. "Seriously, I had no clue she was interested. Addie mentioned it this morning after I left Guest Services. I was in her line at the bank."

"How fortuitous. This changes everything as far as I am concerned. Addie is similar to me. She knows this island like the back of her hand. I couldn't think of a more qualified candidate. Also, her banking skills will come in handy when tasked with collecting money for programs and fees. Thanks, Knox." On impulse, she planted a kiss squarely on his lips.

Knox didn't object, simply kissed her back.

This was their new normal. Unexpected signs of closeness minus the label...for now. "I'll still interview all three. If Addie is on par or a step above, I'll pick her."

"Passports," the word escaped Knox's lips.

"Right. Our final stamp," she replied.

She collected the trash and rose from the table. "The line is long," Cate observed, checking the time on her phone. "Hopefully, it will move fast."

"It should. I'll bet we're not the only ones here on a lunch break," he reasoned.

"Heading to Bait & Switch or back home after this?" In the back of her mind, she was still hung up on what caused his tardiness.

"Home. Uncle Charlie has a virtual checkup at one-thirty this afternoon. If I'm not on the chat with him, nothing important will be discussed. He'll gloss over and say whatever is best for the doctor to hear."

Suddenly, a clear picture formed in Cate's mind about what happened to make Knox act squirrelly, for lack of a better word. "Did Will mention anything about your first job assignment?" She decided to keep the conversation on a relatively conflict-free topic as opposed to digging in the dirt for buried feelings and possible resentments.

"Not at all. Maybe after tonight's big announcement, you could show me around the island. It wouldn't hurt to snap some preliminary photos." He pretended to take a picture with his hands.

"Let's see what my day holds before we firm up any plans." Being this close to Knox was making prioritizing her life that much harder.

"Fair enough," he conceded.

When Cate drew near the front of the line, the nature center employee grabbed her attention.

"Next, please. Make sure you write in your team's name and your own. The more people on your team, the more chances you have to win."

Lucky number seven was how many stamps Cate and Knox earned. The cashier was doing double duty, ringing up the customers and collecting the passports. A sealed box with a slit on top was where the passports needed to go to be eligible to win. They took turns inserting a completed passport and then rang the bell, signaling to all in earshot their two entries had been made.

"I need to head back. Anything else to talk about before we part company?" She was still curious about the details of his and Will's encounter.

"Not that I can think of."

As Cate expected, he didn't dare meet her eye. Instead, he gave her a standard non-committal answer to avoid further questions. She noticed his tense shoulders sagged. He was not ready or prepared to be forthcoming with whatever was bothering him. "I'll see you at the pavilion at five with my fingers crossed for the win," she said in a cheerful voice. She sensed her enthusiasm rubbed off on Knox ever-so-slightly.

He enveloped her in a gentle hug and kissed her on the lips.

"I'm here for you…always." She kissed him back and then slipped away. Her mind was contemplating all she needed to accomplish in a short amount of time.

****

On the short trip back to Uncle Charlie's house, Knox was fully aware Cate was on to him. She could tell when something was bothering him. Today was no exception. He had no time to hash out what happened with Will. Her job was more important right now. The last thing he needed to do was burden her with his issues. Granted, being tugged in different directions was taking a toll. Something had to give, but what?

First priority for the afternoon was Uncle Charlie. Mayor Sam was kind enough to wait until Knox arrived home before heading out. He found the old friends seated at the dining room table, a deck of cards spread out between them.

"Rummy or go fish?" Knox grabbed a seat next to his uncle.

Uncle Charlie shushed him. "I'm about to win." He laid down his hand with a devilish grin to match.

"You beat me again, Charlie. Glad to see you're feeling more like yourself." Mayor Sam collected the cards, slipping them back into the tattered box.

"I appreciate you coming by. Ran into Adeline at the bank," Knox added.

"Funny you should mention her name," Mayor Sam replied.

He quickly surmised that the mayor had a not-so-hidden agenda.

"Adeline's hoping to make a career change," explained Mayor Sam.

"So I've heard." Knox made it easy by explaining what happened with Kelsey and how he already put in a good word with Cate. "She's the newly appointed Guest Services manager. She'll make a good boss." He couldn't help but boast a bit.

"I do appreciate your willingness to help my daughter. You're a fine young man. Thank you, Knox." The mayor placed a light hand on Knox's shoulder and then excused himself, citing some prior commitment at town hall.

Next on the day's agenda was a post-surgery

wellness check. Uncle Charlie's doctor offered video chatting for patients who lived outside Beaufort. Knox signed up for this option, fully aware that getting his uncle to comply would be easier than dragging him to an appointment off the island.

Settled in his favorite corner chair, Uncle Charlie started flipping through the channels for an interesting show. The volume was at its usual, blaring loud enough for the neighbors to hear.

"I'm searching for the pad of paper where we wrote down our questions for the doctor. Do you happen to know where we put it?" Knox rummaged through a pile of old magazines piled on the coffee table.

"Using the 'we' pronoun rather generously, son. I had nothing to do with it. The questions are all yours. Like I told you before, I think this video chat is a total waste of the doctor's time. Oh, here." He withdrew the crumpled list from the side table and handed it to his nephew.

"Thanks." Knox disappeared into the bedroom to fetch his laptop. "Time to get you situated for your 1:30 p.m. telehealth call." He shoved aside the TV tray table in front of his uncle and propped the laptop on a book he borrowed from the bookcase. "Let's review. This is the camera. Focus your attention right here." He pointed to be clear. "Your doctor will appear on the screen. Simply talk like you normally do. No need to yell. The volume will be on full blast. I'll be on the couch if you encounter operating difficulties."

"Or if I skip any of these questions," Uncle Charlie needled him.

Knox laughed. "Yes. I'll be happy to jump in if the

need arises. We have fifteen minutes until we need to log on."

The cell phone in Knox's pocket vibrated. He took it out, not recognizing the number on the screen. "Hello?" he answered. "Yes, this is Knox Price."

Uncle Charlie fussed at him for talking so loud and interrupting his show.

To keep the peace, Knox ducked outside to speak with the caller.

"Hello, Knox. This is Jacque Mitchell, the human resources manager at the National Wildlife Conservation. I'm calling in reference to the full-time position in Washington, D.C. you applied for two months ago. The candidate to whom we extended an offer has declined the position. Since you were one of the finalists, I'm calling to see if you are still interested."

In disbelief over how lucky he was to be in the running again, Knox waited a moment before replying. "Yes, I'm interested in pursuing it."

"Great. Are you available today at four for a phone interview? I realize it's soon, but the hiring manager is insistent on filling this position rather quickly."

"Four o'clock works. And how soon would the job begin, if I were to get the position?" He swallowed hard, trying to contain the excitement bubbling through his veins.

"Four weeks. A shoot is scheduled for Colorado, which explains the urgency. Everything has been booked except the photographer." The manager exchanged contact information with Knox, and she promised to send along the updated job description and benefits package via email. "If you have any further questions, please feel free to reach out to me. Good luck."

With five minutes to go before the telehealth link went live, Knox reappeared in the living room.

"I was hoping you forgot," Uncle Charlie chuckled. "Who was on the phone?"

Knox commandeered the laptop in order to click on the link included in the confirmation email. "A recruiter about a job I applied for a couple of months back. We can talk more about it after the appointment. You ready? Here we go."

Up popped the screen with the doctor seated at his office desk, waiting to see his patient. Surprisingly, Uncle Charlie stuck to the program and asked every question on the list plus a few extras.

The doctor was pleased with how well his patient was progressing and encouraged him to keep up the good work.

When the appointment ended, Knox removed the laptop and tray from his uncle's lap. "What's this about a job?" he said gruffly.

Powering down his laptop, he avoided eye contact with his uncle.

Uncle Charlie frowned. "Aren't you supposed to be helping out the Purdeys? The way I see it, you should fulfill the commitment you already made before taking on something else. Knox, you've been happy here on Gull Island the past week. What's changed?"

Knox stopped what he was doing. "The National Wildlife Conservation has an opening for a photographer based out of D.C. The assignment would be capturing images of wildlife in their natural habitats across the United States. The interview is today at four.

If I land this job, I can prove to my dad once and for all that I have what it takes to be a full-time professional photographer. I have to admit, the timing is less than ideal. But if I pass on it, offers like this will dry up."

"And that's a bad thing why?" Uncle Charlie persisted.

Knox jutted his chin, his fists clenched. "I've spent the last few years building up my resume with prestigious photo shoots with nationally renowned accounts for this type of opportunity. Why would I throw that all away? This is my dream job."

Uncle Charlie eyed his nephew. "Will you run it by Cate?"

"I doubt it. It's happening too fast. Cate is under a lot of stress right now. Mentioning this potential job opportunity would be inconsiderate, to say the least. Plus, I've got to believe I'm not the only one vying for the position. Heck, I probably won't even get it." Knox searched his uncle's face for affirmation.

"And if you do?" Uncle Charlie asked.

"If I do, I'll cross that bridge when I come to it. The start date is nearly a month away. I'll have plenty of time to honor my commitment to you and to the Purdeys," Knox reasoned.

"One last point and I'll drop it for now. In my younger years, I was a lot like you in the sense that I was always searching for the next best thing, rather than embracing what I had at the time. Planning for the future is sensible, I'll grant you that. But, the road to success doesn't always lead you in the right direction. Think about it."

Knox swallowed hard, digesting what his uncle said. "Time for your next dose of pills. What would you

179

like to eat and drink? Can't take the meds on an empty stomach. We learned that the hard way." He threaded a hand through his hair.

"Peanut butter crackers and sweet tea sound good," Uncle Charlie said.

"Coming right up."

After snacking and taking the next dose of medicine, Uncle Charlie retired to the hospital bed for a nap.

Knox drew the drapes to block out the sunshine and tucked him in with a light blanket. His uncle preferred to keep the air-conditioning set at seventy-two degrees. A little warm for Knox, but he never complained. After all, the most important thing was making Uncle Charlie comfortable.

Out in the kitchen, Knox fired up his laptop to do a little research on Purdey & Son. First, he tackled the website and made notes on what he liked and what needed some improvement on a white legal pad he found tucked in a kitchen drawer. He skipped over the current projects because those were the photos he would be replacing. Next he searched for other local contractors and compared their competing digital footprints. From what Knox could decipher, the Purdeys were either on par or excelling in these areas. After he completed an in-depth review, Knox's confidence about effectively lending his talents to Purdey & Son increased exponentially. What made him feel even better was the scope of the Purdey project. If need be, he could easily complete it within a month's time frame.

The time neared three in the afternoon when Knox woke his uncle from his nap. "Rise and shine." He drew back the drapes. Peering outside, he was surprised by the overcast skies. "Is rain in the forecast?"

His uncle struggled to sit up. "The morning weatherman reported a chance of rain. The sky appears ominous, if you ask me. Check your fancy weather app on your phone and see what it has to say." He was able to adjust himself into a seated position without assistance. Next up, he slowly maneuvered each leg over the side of the bed.

"Wow," Knox exclaimed. "I'm impressed."

With little help from Knox, Uncle Charlie returned to the family room and into his recliner. He used the remote controls to power up the television and tune into his all-access news channel. "Nell is stopping by around four with dinner. Would you like me to save you some or do you have other plans? No pressure. We're having pork tenderloin, green beans, and fresh fruit."

Knox rounded up his belongings. "Sounds like a perfect summer meal. I'll take my chances there will be some leftovers. I'm hoping Cate and I will be able to grab something to eat before we check out some recent projects by the Purdeys."

"But what if you two win the scavenger hunt? Won't you be going on the lighthouse tour tonight?"

Uncle Charlie made a good point. "I guess it all depends. Either way, time for me to leave. You still want me to swing by Bait & Switch and make the bank drop before my phone call?" Knox removed his uncle's Clemson ball cap from a hook by the door and placed it backward on his head.

"Absolutely. Get moving before the bank closes, and be careful," his uncle warned.

"Right back at you," he replied. "The door is unlocked." With his personal and professional life in the balance, he had so much to gain or lose. Only time would tell. He inhaled a deep breath and blew out slowly, debating how he wanted the night to end.

Chapter Thirteen

The roads were filled with traffic as beachgoers made their way back from a long day in the sun. The overcast skies sent them home earlier than usual for fear of getting caught in a late day shower. Knox veered away from pedestrians moseying cluelessly into traffic, weighed down with beach chairs, floats, and tired kids.

Entering Bait & Switch, Knox received greetings from the staff with fist bumps and pats on the back. All inquired about Uncle Charlie's progress. Ducking behind the front counter, he gathered the big bills and swiped the green deposit pouch. Heading to the backroom, he bumped into Eliza who was dropping off the reservation book. All the businesses were closing early today for the grand drawing.

"Just the man I was looking for." She waved the book in the air.

Knox hesitated a moment, torn between grabbing the cat's tin of food and chatting with Eliza. If he wanted to squeeze everything in by five, he didn't have much time to waste on small talk. "Hey, Eliza. Would you mind taking the book upstairs? My uncle has me running over to the bank before meeting everyone at the pavilion."

"Sure. No problem. After I get done here, I'm going home to change before heading over to help Will," she explained.

"Thanks, Eliza." He hurried down the hallway.

"Knox, wait," Eliza shouted.

He stopped dead in his tracks. "Yes?" He quickly glanced at his watch.

"I keep forgetting to ask you. My mother would like to stop by to see Uncle Charlie late this afternoon." She toyed with her hair.

"Fine," he answered curtly.

"She figured we'd all be busy with the scavenger hunt," she continued.

"Right. Good idea," he commented, trying to slip away.

"Didn't want him to feel left out," Eliza added.

Knox paused mid-step. "Sure."

"Maybe around four or a little after? Would that be a good time for her to visit?" She pressed on.

"Yes," he said.

"Oh, she also was concerned about him trying to get to the front door. She would hate to be the reason for him falling. Should she call ahead or maybe text you when she leaves the house?" Eliza asked.

"No, I won't be there anyway. I've got a phone interview at four, and Nell is coming by with supper so she can open the door and let her in. It works fine," he blurted, his frustration getting the better of him.

As soon as the words escaped his lips, Knox felt his stomach clench. Eliza's gape said it all. Instantly, the immediate need for damage control stopped him from going into detail. Like he told his uncle, he might not land the job. If he explained himself to Eliza, he was all but admitting he had one foot off the island. "I'll see you at the pavilion for the big announcement." Simple and direct. He shuffled his feet waiting for her reaction.

"Yes. Yes, you will." Her expression hardened.

To clear his head, Knox headed over to the bank, dodging the scattering raindrops. The stop would be brief, no need to go inside. He'd utilize the night drop instead of wasting time standing in line. When he arrived, the parking lot was nearly empty. He supposed the majority of patrons were making their way to the pavilion. Fewer than three minutes passed as he walked up, opened the green pouch, and deposited the plastic bag inside containing wads of bills held together with a deposit slip and rubber band. He wiped the raindrops from his brow, and then inserted the key into the cart. With a light foot and a heavy heart, he set out on his way.

Now with his responsibilities taken care of, he shifted his focus to his interview. If it weren't for the drizzling rain, the perfect place to take the call would have been the marina. There he had once decided to leave Gull Island, an intersection between the life he knew and the one he dreamed of. Revisiting it underscored the decision he needed to make. Luckily, the covered pier was quiet at this time of day, so he sat on one of the wooden benches and waited for the call. At four on the dot, his phone rang. "Hello," he said politely. "Yes, now is the perfect time to talk."

****

Driving over to the pavilion after the interview, Knox replayed the conversation in his head. He answered all the technical questions about photography and lighting with ease. When the topic switched to coping with the stress attached to the job, Knox avoided anything too personal in his responses. Never had he associated taking photographs with stress. If anything, he used photography to escape from the stresses of day-to-day life. The biggest takeaway from the conversation was his lack of excitement about the position. Part of it had to do with being the company's second choice, its consolation prize. The other was the interviewer's sense of urgency to fill it. Life-changing decisions were to be made with careful consideration, not in a hurry.

Although he welcomed the amazing opportunity, Knox realized his friends and Cate might see it differently. While he couldn't undo the harm caused by his careless slip to Eliza, he could prepare himself for the fallout. He needed to get his head on straight.

The steady precipitation on his windshield impeded his view. Regardless, he navigated his way around the island to get where he was going. He kept an eye out for his favorite deer, Theo, but the buck was nowhere in sight. Probably hunkered down with the herd until the rain shower passed. Knox remembered how as a kid, he liked to search for their hideouts.

The pavilion was a happening place. He could hear loud music a block or two away. When he rounded the corner, Knox bumped into a large crowd of people of varying ages. The clam-like structure of the pavilion was big enough to provide coverage for the band onstage and those gathered in front who wanted to keep dry. Knox noticed small clusters of teens undeterred by the rain, which was slowly letting up. Parents congregated by the playground equipment, observing their kids dart between the raindrops for a quick turn on the slide. He parked his cart in his usual space, not far from Will's. With the bright orange Clemson rain tarp, his friend's cart was easy to recognize.

Taking a deep breath of courage, he ventured out to find his friends and pay the price for his slip of tongue. Knox first located Will, the MC for the event, who stood in front of the band on the temporary stage. He listened to his friend rattle off the sponsors' names and promised the crowd the light rain would pass momentarily. Eliza was not far from him, shuffling through a small stack of papers. Cate was nowhere to be found, which surprised him. He expected her to be glued to her friend's side, helping with last-minute emergencies and whatnot. He scoured the crowd in search of Jackson's tall frame and wound up empty-handed. Pacing toward the food vendors lined up in a row, he continued to scan the scene for any sign of his girlfriend.

"There you are," Cate shouted from somewhere behind.

Knox followed in the direction of her voice, easily spotting her in a bright yellow rain slicker. He took a steadying breath, ready to answer whatever questions she might have about his job interview. From the cheerful grin on her face, he could tell Eliza hadn't shared his news…yet. Stepping toward her, Knox opened his arms and drew her into a bear hug. Lifting her chin with the cup of his hand, he gently kissed her lips, savoring the cherry taste. "Cherry snow-cone?" he guessed.

"Is it that obvious?" she laughed.

Hand in hand, Knox led her in the general direction of the crowd. When he neared the stage, Cate waved hello to Eliza but didn't venture over to where she was standing.

Eliza reciprocated the wave and acknowledged

Knox with a slight nod of her chin.

"We don't want to seem too cozy with the officials, especially if we win." She tugged on his arm.

"Smart," Knox agreed, secretly happy to avoid having an uncomfortable conversation with their mutual friend.

A few minutes before five, the crowd swelled around the staging area.

"May I have your attention, please?" Will's deep voice commanded the crowd.

Knox eyed Mayor Sam and Nell quietly approaching, weaving in and out of groups of friends to make their way to the front. Will mentioned how the mayor volunteered to draw the passport from the box of entries. "Who better to impartially select the prizewinner than the leading dignitary of the island?" Will gloated.

"The rain stopped, just as Will predicted," Knox said quietly to Cate.

"It sure did. The sky is slightly overcast, but I see a hint of sunshine trying to peek out." She pointed skyward.

"Welcome to the third annual Gull Island Scavenger Hunt benefitting the Lowcountry Conservation Fund. My name is Will Purdey, the founder and organizer of the event and a local Gull Islander." He clasped his hands behind his back. "Competition was fierce this year with over two hundred and fifty entries and a little under two hundred completions. I'd like to thank our local sponsors, too many to name, who take part in this family event. Their businesses are featured on the posters displayed around the pavilion. Please stop by and thank them for their support by buying locally. Also, we have food trucks this year, parked alongside the pavilion. If you're hungry, I invite you to sample some of our Lowcountry favorites."

On cue, Knox spied Mayor Sam leaving Nell's side and moving closer. His friend orchestrated the day's events down to the very last detail. His attention focused on Eliza.

She withdrew a large box from under a folding table and set it down in front of her boyfriend.

"I'd like to introduce Mayor Sam Heyward, who will draw the winning entry. The grand prize is a private candlelight tour of the lighthouse, which is closed to the public. A rare glimpse into the past, courtesy of the Gull Island Historical Society. Our volunteers are there now preparing for this exclusive behind-the-scenes tour. So, without further ado, Mayor Sam, will you please join me?"

"Will's giving the box a good shake," Cate observed.

"Oh look, Mayor Sam is assuming his position," Knox commented in a voice raised over the loud chatter from the excited crowd.

Mayor Sam carefully lifted the lid of the box and ceremoniously inserted his arm shoulder-deep to fish out the winning entry. After a bit of showmanship, he held up one lucky passport for the crowd to see. Passing it over to Will, he stepped aside so the crowd could hear the name of the lucky team.

"And the winner is…Team Hip, Hip, Hooray!"

Cate's flailing arms practically knocked Knox off his feet.

Laughter erupted from those standing close by,

witnessing her overzealous behavior.

Knox saved face by jumping from one foot to another, mimicking a prize fighter.

"Team Hip, Hip, Hooray, please come on up for the presentation of the grand prize," announced Will, all businesslike.

Knox was amused with his friend speaking as if he had no idea who the team members were. If nothing else, Will demonstrated his impartiality by remaining seemingly neutral over the personal connection to his circle of friends.

Cate grabbed Knox's hand and dragged him through the thick crowd.

Mayor Sam slapped Knox on the back, congratulating him for a job well done.

Knox overheard Nell whispering something in Cate's ear about a romantic evening.

On stage, Will hugged Cate in a friendly manner and extended a hand to Knox, without locking gazes.

Uh, oh, news travels fast. Knox stepped aside, allowing Eliza room to pass by with a three-foot, cut-out replica of the lighthouse on her way to Will. He stepped back in position next to Cate just in time for Will to hand them the prop.

"Please stand over here for the photo op," Will pointed toward the photographer.

On the count of three, Knox and Cate smiled as the photographer from the local newspaper snapped a handful of shots documenting this year's winning team. Knox winced at what was coming next. Just on the off-chance Eliza hadn't told Will the news, he decided to let his friend speak first. He debated whether to blame the heat or his frazzled nerves for the sweat dripping down his back, adding to his unabated discomfort.

"If you had no intention of helping me and my dad, you should have just said so. Why did I have to hear from Eliza you had a job interview today? The Knox I grew up with would have filled me in first," he pointed out, with a drizzle of spit unintentionally spewing from his lips.

"Whoa." Knox held up his hand. "Let me explain."

Will forged on. "More importantly, what did Cate say when you told her?"

Knox lowered his head. Dread had been growing in him all day.

"Really, Knox? I told Eliza you'd never interview for a job without discussing it with Cate first because you two are a couple again. But Eliza was not having it." Will paced back and forth, his hands flailing in the air. "She guessed Cate was completely in the dark. To think, I am the one who encouraged Cate to let you back into her life. I should have minded my own business."

"It all happened so fast, really fast. As in today. The headhunter called and scheduled me for a phone interview this afternoon. No prep time. No warning. Let's not make more out of it. Like I told Uncle Charlie, I probably won't get the job anyway." He tried to downplay it.

"And when you do, because they'd be dumb not to hire you since you're unbelievably talented, when would you start?" asked Will.

"My first photo shoot would be in a month, which means I'll have plenty of time to complete the work for Purdey & Son and get my uncle back on his feet," Knox reasoned.

"And Cate?" Will shuffled his feet.

"I wasn't planning to tell her because she's under a lot of stress starting her new job and hiring her replacement. It would be selfish to add this to her plate." Knox tucked his hands into his pockets.

Will exhaled noisily through pursed lips. "I might be wrong, but I don't think Cate's going to see it that way."

The hurt in Will's eyes made Knox feel guilty about not being transparent with his friends. "For what it's worth, I haven't had time to process it myself, much less explain to everyone else what's going on. I didn't mean to let it slip to Eliza the way I did. I planned to talk to you all about it."

"I get it," answered Will. "It caught me by surprise, and I probably overreacted, but I was coming from a good place. You need to get your head on straight and start thinking about what you want to do. If that means taking this job, if offered, then go for it. They'd be lucky to get you. I'm not going to lie, though. I was hoping this time you'd stay for good."

A voice over the loudspeaker summoned Will to the welcome area.

"That's me." Will forced a smile.

"You better go," Knox replied. "I'm sorry. I should have handled this better."

"Let me offer you some free advice, my friend. Don't make the same mistake again. Cate deserves to know the truth. She loves you, Knox." Will departed, tending to his many responsibilities, with Eliza paying close attention in the background.

Luckily, Cate was facing the opposite direction or else she would have witnessed their serious discussion.

Eliza's furrowed brow deepened Knox's guilt for allowing himself to be in this position. If he heeded his uncle's warning, he'd be anticipating a romantic evening with his girlfriend, instead of figuring out a way to keep her from being hurt again by his careless behavior.

****

Cate was beyond excited about winning the lighthouse tour. The National Register of Historic Places recently made renovations, and seeing them up close with Knox by her side sweetened the win. The noise of the crowd made it difficult for Cate to chat with Eliza, especially with people constantly interrupting them to congratulate her on the lucky win. She wanted to ask her friend about the lighthouse's restoration.

"Congratulations." Will side-hugged her, planting a light kiss on her cheek.

"Thanks, Will. I can't wait for the candlelight tour. Have you seen Knox? He seems to have disappeared." Cate craned her neck, scanning the crowd in both directions.

"I think I see him over there talking to Jackson." He tilted his head in the direction.

Cate caught sight of Knox and her brother near the information booth. "Oh, good. I was hoping Jackson could drive my cart back to the house. Will you be at the lighthouse tonight?"

"And crash your private tour? Heck, no. I'll be at home on the couch with the remote in my hand." He gave a half-smile.

"And I will be sitting next to him." Eliza looped her arm into his.

"Rightfully so. Congratulations, again. Lots of money raised for the Lowcountry Conservation Fund." Her mouth curved into a smile.

"Hello, sis." Jackson approached from behind with Knox. "I hear congratulations are in order."

"Thanks. Are you ready for tomorrow's meet?" Cate asked.

"Ready as I'll ever be." He chewed on his bottom lip.

"Before we head to the lighthouse, Knox and I are taking a quick side trip. He's hoping to get a head start on his project for the Purdeys. If all goes as planned, this guy here," she poked Knox's stomach, "will become a bona fide employee of Purdey & Son in the not-so-distant future."

"Want to take my cart?" Knox quickly asked.

"If you're okay with my driving. Easier for you to take pictures if I'm navigating the road." Cate didn't miss a beat.

"No problem," said Knox.

Cate dangled the key in the air. "Do you mind driving this other cart home?"

"I figured as much." Jackson swiped the keychain. "Have fun. I'll see you later."

The group was saying their goodbyes, parting ways for the night, when Mayor Sam and Nell hurried toward them.

"Wait. Please don't leave yet," Mayor Sam insisted. When they joined the group, he continued. "We're lucky to have found all of you in one place. Nell and I would like to invite you to join us tomorrow at seven for a sunset cruise on our boat. Celebrating the success of this year's scavenger hunt and, of course, the winning team. Talk among yourselves and let us know in the morning. Job well done, Will."

"Thank you. I had a good team of helpers." Will shared the praise.

Mayor Sam's attention was diverted by a colleague heading in his direction. "Councilman," he called out.

"Duty calls," Nell announced to the group. "We hope you're able to join us."

Cate played with her hair, eyes and ears alert. She grabbed Knox's hand and squeezed.

Eliza spoke to Will in a hushed tone. "Another reason why we shouldn't go to Charleston for the art show."

"What do you mean another reason?" Cate stepped closer to Eliza. "You don't want to miss an opportunity to advance your career."

"We planned to stay with my aunt and uncle, but their schedule changed. I was supposed to find a hotel for Saturday night, but I completely forgot." Will shrugged.

Eliza reached for his hand. "Why don't we just stay here this weekend? Cate could use an extra set of hands in the office, and you've worked so hard to make this event a huge success. You deserve the chance to celebrate, and what better way than out on the water at sunset. There will be ample opportunities to meet the owner of the gallery, especially with your uncle's connection. Besides, you've been promising me a boat ride. Here's your chance to make good on your promise."

"Are you sure?" Will held both of her hands.

Eliza rose on her tippy toes and kissed him lightly on the lips. "Yes, I am." Then she faced Cate. "I'll always have your back, boss lady."

"Thanks for sticking around. When I need you most, you're always there." Cate softened her gaze.

"All settled," Knox said. "Will, how about you call Mayor Sam in the morning and let him know we're all in?"

****

After stopping for tacos, Cate and Knox set out in the cart to explore the island. She couldn't wait to show him the latest projects constructed by Purdey & Son and gauge his reaction. She had a feeling he'd be intrigued with how the architecture evolved since his living here. Cate made small talk about the award ceremony and their good fortune. Along the lesser-known streets, she pointed out new homes built by Purdey & Son. "See how the position of the setting sun frames the houses in streaks of reds and pinks." She was pleased Knox seemed mesmerized with what he was seeing.

He hopped out of the cart several times to get the perfect angle highlighting the architecture and the beauty of the island.

"The Purdeys' work includes a variety of building techniques which focus on minimizing negative ecological impact," she explained. "Their creative use of renewable and salvaged materials gives each home uniqueness." Cate hoped he would capture this innovation in his photographs. Cate looped back around to get another view of two houses in particular.

"The right balance of building and nature makes a house feel more like a home," he added.

"Mind if I take a peek at some of your shots? I'm fascinated by the process," Cate asked.

Knox willingly obliged.

In her way of thinking, they both were tasked with this project, not just him. "Do you have enough images to work with?"

He nodded. "I think so. Might as well head back to Grammy's house. I imagine you'll want to change and catch up with Jackson while you are there, so how about I take the cart and be back around a quarter to eight? That should leave us plenty of time to get to the lighthouse."

"That works," Cate replied. "Jackson has to get good times tomorrow in order to qualify for the summer state meet. I'm pretty sure he was carb-loading today, but he still needs hydration and plenty of rest to prepare for the morning. It won't hurt for him to be reminded of this by his big sister."

Cate glanced at her phone for a time check. If she would make this tight turnaround, every minute counted. After giving Knox a quick peck on the cheek, she hopped out of the cart, determined to be dressed and ready to roll with time to spare. A lofty goal, but well within her grasp if she put her mind to it.

With vigor, Cate darted into the bathroom for a second shower of the day. With no time for a blow dry, she tied an elastic in her hair. With a quick flick of her wrist, she created a chic messy bun. She wanted to wear a simple outfit, something relaxed and effortless, as if she wasn't trying too hard. She picked a sleeveless maxi dress with the tags still on, bought for a special occasion like tonight. Heading back to the bathroom, she carefully applied makeup and a neutral gloss on her lips. Grabbing tiny amethyst studs off the dresser and her favorite arrow necklace, her style was complete with ten minutes to spare.

On her way out, she noticed her library book on the side table in the family room. Cate's schedule the past few days left barely any time to keep up with the fictional romance of Abby and Beau. She picked it up, pondering how she could ever feel fulfilled with turning pages when her real Beau was only moments away. She shelved it in its rightful place. Maybe tonight was a sign to put away the make-believe world she was living in and find her own everlasting love.

Chapter Fourteen

Standing outside ready to be picked up, Cate was giddy with excitement for the romantic evening about to unfold. The brief knowledge about the historical background of the lighthouse would make for a good conversation starter for the ride over. Online she'd read stories about different lightkeepers who lived there over the centuries. She hoped the docent in charge of their tour would shed some light on the lighthouse's interesting history.

Knox arrived right on time.

Cate was standing there as promised. She could tell by his sweet smile her promptness pleased him. Cate slid into the front seat of the cart, careful to gather her maxi dress so it wouldn't get caught in a wheel.

"You are beautiful," he professed barely above a whisper.

One of the things Cate loved most about Knox was his sincerity. For as long as she had known him, he said what he truly meant.

"Are you excited to get a behind-the-scenes tour of the lighthouse?" Knox backed out of the driveway and onto the road.

Cate was happy to share her knowledge of the historic landmark, especially the part about the lightkeeper.

"With the rain from earlier, the fog will be thick

Jennifer Vido

tonight. You won't be scared, will you?" he teased.
"There might be ghosts lurking."

"I have you to protect me," she answered, slipping
her left hand into his right. She held it tightly for the
remainder of the drive. Upon approach to the
lighthouse, Cate was blown away by the sea of
luminary bags with flameless candles lighting the
walkway. "Seeing the lighthouse at night is a whole
different experience, as is getting to go inside," she
bubbled over with excitement. "Look at the very top, a
beacon of light is shining down over the water." She
could only imagine how amazing she'd feel when they
crossed the threshold.

Knox parked near the door, and he hurried to
Cate's side of the cart as she got out.

Walking in tandem toward the entrance, she liked
the feel of his protective hand on the small of her back,
guiding her along the way.

Standing out front was a slender, older gentleman,
dressed in period clothing from the eighteen hundreds,
holding a tray with two drinks. "Good evening." He
swiftly handed each a glass of champagne. "My name is
Edward, and I have the pleasure of being your guide
tonight. Please be my guest." He stepped aside and
ushered them into the lighthouse. Inside the tower, the
guide pointed out the masonry and brick used to
construct the white painted walls.

Despite the humidity, the air was cool inside. A
spiraling staircase climbed toward the sky. "Good thing
I wore sensible shoes," Cate spoke to Knox in a hushed
tone, careful not to appear rude or insensitive to the
docent. "This climb to the top is like an intense cardio
workout." Cate's heart pounded in her ears, quite

200

possibly the effect of taking the stairs too rapidly or the presence of Knox's close proximity in the narrow tower.

"The 360-degree view of Gull Island is breathtaking with miles of marsh and beaches," Knox raved at the pinnacle. The landing was cramped with barely enough room for two people to stand in front of each other.

"I'll take your word for it." Cate averted her gaze from the sight. The low wall and spindly railing made her dizzy.

Knox braved the fog and wind to capture the best view. Sticking his head over the railing, he peered over the edge, and then slowly adjusted his attention.

She drew in a quick breath when she caught him staring, the intensity of his gaze sending her heart aflutter.

"In the mid-eighteen hundreds, a deadly hurricane hit the island, causing destruction to the original lighthouse," the docent explained. "Shortly after the Civil War, the lighthouse was rebuilt. It has been home to numerous keepers, all with interesting stories to tell. Caring for the light and lens were the lighthouse keepers' main duties. Heroic rescues in teeming waters were also a mainstay of the job.

"One particular story comes to mind. Ruth Amos was a pretty young lady whose father intended for her to marry the town's physician. Unfortunately for him, Ruth set her heart on Jonathan Pearce, the lightkeeper. When Mr. Amos got wind of their romance, he sent her off to live with a distant cousin. Before she left, Jonathan professed his undying love and promised to wait to marry until her return. He planted Ruth's favorite azaleas around the keeper's cottage to remember her by. Every spring the flowers' fragrant scent kept her memory alive."

"Isn't that so romantic?" Cate whispered in Knox's ear.

Knox hugged her closer.

Edward smiled at the couple and continued with the story.

"Years passed and Ruth's father eventually passed away. Jonathan had all but given up hope, resigned to living alone in the lighthouse. One day as he was weeding the garden, a horse-drawn carriage approached. He put aside his trowel and properly greeted the visitor. As the driver helped a woman out of the buggy, he instantly recognized Ruth. She found her way back to Gull Island and came to see if her one true love was still waiting.

"Jonathan kept true to his word and never loved another. The two married and grew old together, living a quiet life tending the lighthouse. It goes to show, no matter distance or circumstances, true love conquers all," he affirmed.

Cate tilted her chin up just as Knox kissed her gently on the lips.

He placed his hand on the small of her back, escorting her down the steps to a small table set with white linens, a centerpiece of floating camellias in a crystal bowl, and a scattering of Lowcountry desserts, including tiny pecan tarts, petit fours, and cream cheese brownie bites.

The docent invited them to take a seat at the table. "And this is where the tour ends. I encourage you to stay on the grounds as long as you like, after sampling these treats. Congratulations on your lucky win. I hope you have enjoyed this tour."

Knox had been quiet most of the night, which Cate attributed to his being in awe of the lighthouse.

"Did you have a good time?" Knox squished closer outside on a bench surrounded by the luminaries.

Cate's pulse quickened. This was the part she had been waiting for all night. She had difficulty reading him because he surely wasn't acting like himself. In her mind, she debated whether he would tell her he loved her or that he was making Gull Island his permanent home. Maybe both. "We need to talk about something," he began. "I received a phone call earlier today." He parted his lips.

Cate was thrown a bit. She didn't know how a phone call could factor into this. but she was willing to listen. "Go on," she urged.

He cleared his throat.

Here we go, she inwardly cheered.

"I can't find an easy way to say this, Cate." He curled the edge of the napkin, focusing his attention on the silverware.

She stared, confused as to where he was going with the conversation. Neither of her scenarios played out like this. "I don't understand," she mumbled, searching his eyes for answers.

"The National Wildlife Conservation in Washington, D.C. has an opening for a full-time staff photographer. I interviewed for the position this afternoon."

Cate inhaled a sharp breath, turning her head aside.

****

Sitting in his idling truck, Knox sipped piping hot

coffee from a travel mug, waiting for Jackson to come out of the house. Keeping his distance from Cate seemed like the sensible thing to do. The hot liquid trickled down his throat, warming his insides despite feeling cold and alone. He inspected the clothes he was wearing, mismatched and wrinkled, but shrugged it off as unimportant. Of much greater importance was the way yesterday ended and what today would bring. The news of his job interview cut Cate to the quick. If only she said something, anything. Her stillness was no match for his desperation to make things right. Unlike years ago, this time she was the one who backed away. He lost the argument without having a chance to plead his case.

A slamming front door reverberated from the familiar yellow beach cottage. On the off-chance Cate made an appearance, Knox kept his gaze steady and alert.

Jackson slung his team-issued bag over his shoulder as he shuffled half-asleep toward the truck. When he hoisted himself up into the cab, he greeted Knox like usual.

Either Jackson was laser focused on the meet, or he had no clue about Knox's job interview. Both options worked for the time being.

Jackson unzipped his bag. "I packed this yesterday in a rush before heading to the pavilion. It'll take me just a second to double-check I have everything."

"Take your time," Knox replied, thankful to stick around a little longer in the hope of seeing Cate.

"Suits, goggles, caps, towels, protein bars, and a bottle of water. Oh, and I've got my headphones to listen to pump-up music before I swim. I'm set."

Jackson zipped it back up and stuffed it on the floor next to his feet.

Knox slowly backed the truck out onto the road, careful to avoid cyclists or early risers before shifting into drive. "The ride is about three hours. If you feel like napping, I don't mind. I have a couple of podcasts to keep me company."

"What time do you think we'll be stopping for breakfast?" Jackson fiddled with the seatbelt.

"Probably in an hour and a half. There shouldn't be much traffic on a Saturday morning," Knox guesstimated.

The two made small talk until Jackson drifted off to sleep.

Knox opted for a sports podcast to pass the time and not have to think of how much he'd hurt Cate again.

At breakfast, the local dive was crowded, which Knox hadn't anticipated. Rather than wait for a table, they decided to eat at the counter. Major league baseball was the topic of discussion, the Braves being their team. Anything was better than rehashing his date with Cate last night.

The qualifying meet was being held at University of South Carolina's natatorium. Ample parking for the large crowd gathered for the event.

Seeing as Knox was unfamiliar with the day's format, Jackson provided a crash course on how to read a heat sheet and match it to the scoreboard. "I'll be swimming in three events—the 200-yard medley relay, the 100-yard butterfly, and 100-yard backstroke."

"OK, let's make a plan where to meet afterward to avoid getting swallowed in the crowd," suggested

Knox.

"How about outside near the entrance? I spied a bicycle rack on our way into the building. I'll hang out there until you surface." He shifted from one foot to the other.

"That works. Good luck, swim fast, and breathe later," he quipped, giving Jackson a reassuring squeeze on the shoulder. Knox headed to the bleachers, which were filled with parents using the swimmers' warm-up time to mark their heat sheets, chat with other team parents, and take care of other commitments via phone while waiting for their kids to compete. Knox planned to use this time to scroll through the photographs he took last night until his phone rang. "Hey, Dad. Surprised to hear from you this early on a Saturday. No golf today?" He turned a corner in search of a quiet spot.

"Pouring rain. I'm sitting at home alone with my coffee and newspaper. Your mother just left for her yoga class. Just calling my favorite son. Seeing how rehab is going with Charlie. Are you two sick of each other yet?"

His father could try as he might to pass off this call as an impromptu check-in, but Knox understood his talk had Uncle Charlie written all over it. "My interview with the National Wildlife Conservation fared well. I assume that's why we are having this conversation early in the morning."

"Your uncle mentioned the job is in D.C. or at least your office would be there. A staff photographer rarely is in a brick-and-mortar office. Lots of traveling in your future, son. But, I'm not telling you anything you don't already know. Quite frankly, I'm surprised to learn of your interest in D.C. I might be able to help you land a job with less travel and a more stable work environment." His father spat out names of potential employers.

"Stop right there." Knox's frustration with the one-sided conversation got the better of him. Distracted by the loud roar of the crowd, he scooted down the hallway and slipped into an empty storage room.

"That's fine, son. If you need to think about it more and then call me back, I'm available all day." His father was completely oblivious to Knox.

To avoid any unnecessary conflict, Knox responded on an even keel. "Thanks for the offer, Dad, but this is my dream job. I've been working internationally as a sought-after freelance photographer for quite some time now, which led me to this opportunity."

"And what about Cate? I can't believe she would be too thrilled about your moving away again."

Knox was surprised to hear him mention her name. He was still wrapping his head around that part of the equation. "I appreciate your willingness to help me find a suitable position, but we have differing opinions on what that might be. Honestly, I thought you were calling to say how proud you were of me." Silence on the other end signaled his dad's disapproval. "Maybe we should continue this some other time," Knox offered. He could hear his father shuffling newspapers.

"You might find this hard to believe, but I've always been proud of you, no matter what job you've held."

"You have?" Knox's voice betrayed his disbelief.

"These past couple of years you've been hiding

behind a lens, traveling all over the place with no sense of purpose in your life. When Uncle Charlie called, both your mother and I believed what better place than Gull Island for you to spend some time figuring out what makes you happy."

"You sent me here?" He continued before letting his father have a chance to speak. "You did not. I made the decision completely on my own because I knew in my heart, I belonged here."

"Undoubtedly, yes. You do belong there," he affirmed.

"Kevin, I'm home."

Knox could hear the faint sound of his mother saying something about forgetting to register. "Dad?" He could tell his father covered the phone with his hand.

"Sorry, son. Your mother distracted me for a moment. Not enough space for her in class."

"Dad, I need to go," Knox insisted. "I'm with Jackson at his swim meet in Columbia. He is due up on the block soon."

"Oh. Is Cate with you?" he asked.

"No. Just the two of us. I volunteered to take him," Knox clarified.

"Well, don't let me keep you," his father urged. "Knox, I'm glad we talked."

"Me, too." Knox promised to give some serious reflection about taking the position, if offered. If nothing else, his father gave him a new perspective on more than just the job.

Making his way back to the viewing area, Knox was surprised at how loud the spectators were when the swimmers were in the water. The high energy and intensity of the competition pervaded the crowd. He searched the pool deck until he located Jackson, and when he finally caught his eye, he gave him a thumbs-up.

The morning flew by. Jackson's relay team placed in the top ten, with his split being two seconds off his seed time. In his individual races, he barely made the top twenty, not enough to qualify for the state meet. Truth be told, Knox was expecting Jackson to qualify in all his events, possibly even the top three. He wondered if something was up with Jackson. With plans to swim in college, Jackson couldn't afford to miss the mark at qualifying meets such as this one.

On schedule with Jackson's estimation, Knox met him at the designated spot, and they were in the truck heading back to Gull Island by two. Jackson appeared the same as he had when he climbed in that morning, sluggish and half-awake.

"How about we stop for a quick bite to eat when we get near Beaufort? I've got a popular food truck in mind known for its culinary spin on fish tacos," Knox suggested.

"I'm in." replied the hungry teenager with a bottomless pit for a stomach.

It must have been ten minutes or so before Jackson passed out from exhaustion. Leaning up against the door, his head was tilted back with his mouth wide-open, as if he just pulled an all-nighter.

Knox used the open road to weigh his options. Hearing his father's pride in him swelled his heart with happiness. When his dad first sprung the news of Uncle Charlie's surgery, Knox didn't question if, but when, he would arrive on Gull Island to help. Little did he realize at the time something more was drawing him back to the place he called home.

Jackson started to stir near Beaufort.

Knox tapped him on the shoulder. "Wake up, dude. Almost time to stop for a late lunch. Are you still hungry?"

Jackson stretched his long arms overhead. "I'm starving. Let me see if I can figure out what their specials are today." He searched on his phone.

"I'm debating if I'm ordering two or three tacos." Knox rocked his head back and forth.

"Always three," Jackson insisted. "We're in luck. Good day for a street taco. Listen up. Here are the choices: Mojito Shrimp, Blackened Mahi Mahi with Sriracha, and Cilantro Lime Flounder. Can't go wrong with any of them. Personally, I like to use mahi mahi when I make tacos. The firmness of the fish works well with the slaw. It soaks up the spices, giving it a kick with every bite."

"Spoken like a master chef," joked Knox. With ten minutes to go, he decided to broach the topic of Jackson's swimming career, or lack thereof. "Sorry you didn't qualify for state. I bet you're disappointed."

"Tough competition. Thanks for coming, though. I appreciate the company." Jackson gave a lopsided grin.

"What's the next step? Do you figure out what's slowing you down and tweak your stroke?" He glanced in Jackson's direction.

"Season is over for me. I'll use the short break to do some serious thinking. Probably hang out with my friends at the beach." Jackson messed with a string from the hem of his athletic shorts.

"Do you have a speed coach willing to help you in

the off-season?" Knox sensed Jackson's uneasiness with their discussion.

"Not sure if it'll fix the issue." He tugged at the single strand.

"Aw, don't give up so easily. If you need me to time you or be your workout buddy, I'd be happy to help," Knox offered.

Jackson ripped the thread right off the shorts. "I've been thinking about my future. Researched schools in a three-hour radius and scholarship opportunities for students like me," he began.

"I'm amazed by your attempt at adulting," Knox commented. "Go on."

"I'd like to attend culinary school. Open a restaurant on Gull Island one day," Jackson blurted.

"Wow. I didn't see that coming. Does Cate know?" Knox eased into a spot near the waterfront.

"Not exactly." Jackson flashed a smile. "That's where you come in. I was hoping maybe you could slip it into a conversation. Soften the blow. I don't want to disappoint my sister."

The last thing Knox wanted to do was burst Cate's bubble about Jackson's promising swimming career. He shut off the ignition. "If I have learned anything, honesty works best, especially with your sister."

"But what if she thinks my idea is dumb?" Jackson implored with a raised pitch in his voice.

"If you want to be a chef, go make it happen. Don't second-guess yourself. If you know, you know. Somehow I don't think this news will be a big surprise to Cate or your parents. Personally speaking, I can't wait to eat at your restaurant."

"So does this mean you'll tell her?" he said, eyes

opened wide.

Knox placed his hand on Jackson's shoulder. "No, but I'll support you when you do."

The irony of the conversation didn't go unnoticed by Knox. He, too, kept secrets from Cate, causing undue hurt because he wasn't brave enough to come clean. Hiding his feelings was the easy way out; yet now he had the chance to make good on what he had known all along—Cate deserved his unbridled love and respect. Now if only he could figure out if she was open to accepting it.

****

Guest Services wouldn't be open for another half hour, yet Cate had the background music playing from the overhead speakers and the inside lights already on. Seated at her office desk, she was busy reviewing resumes for the upcoming interviews. Eliza was keeping her company and organizing the arrival packets in alphabetical order and by type of rental, either home or villa. Homemade lemonade, sweet tea, and cookies were neatly arranged on the welcoming table ready to meet the guests when they arrived. The typical Saturday morning routine might have seemed the same, but in reality, today was anything but normal.

"I knew about Knox's interview. I'm sorry I didn't text you as soon as I found out," Eliza confessed.

"Don't worry about it. You're not to blame for his transgression. What I have a hard time understanding is why Knox didn't say something or even text me. Granted the job opportunity literally fell in his lap yesterday. Who wouldn't be flattered to be considered for such a prestigious position, traveling all over the United States and being featured on a national level?"

The words sounded differently when spoken than when she rehearsed them in her head. His choice to leave her in the dark spoke volumes about their relationship, fueling her anger and disappointment. This was not how she envisioned their second chance at love. "A game changer for his career," she mumbled.

"He said he wanted to give your relationship a second chance. He can't up and leave now, especially with how well you two are getting along," Eliza reasoned. "Plus, he made a commitment to Purdey & Son to help with their marketing. Walking away from Will and his dad would be a mistake, especially seeing how good a friend Will has been to him over the years."

Cate hugged her friend. "I can't be the reason for him not following his dream."

Chapter Fifteen

When nine o'clock rolled around, Cate was in a better head space. A steady stream of departures flowed through the office, settling bills and returning rental keys, which Eliza handled on her own. Meanwhile, Cate was in her office, conducting interviews for the open position.

The first candidate was a middle-aged woman, highly recommended by the corporate office. Newly retired, she and her husband relocated to Gull Island from the Jersey Shore. Familiar with beach living, she proved to be quite well-versed in vacation rentals.

"How might you suggest improvements to Gull Island?" Cate took copious notes.

"Implementing the sale of beach badges to generate additional income would be a good start," she suggested. "Also, have you ever considered hiring undercover cops to patrol the beach to catch underage drinkers?"

"I appreciate your enthusiasm and go-getter attitude." Cate knew in actuality a less high-strung candidate would be a better fit for the office.

The second candidate's CV was light on experience because most consisted of school volunteer opportunities. A recent high school graduate, she planned on enrolling at the community college in the fall. An islander, she was well-informed about all the island offered to out-of-town visitors. Cate was taking a liking to her.

"What skills do you have that would make you a good fit for this position?" Cate readied her pen to record her answer.

"Well, I'm a third-generation Sagittarius, and we are known for being really good with people," she spoke with conviction.

Suppressing her amusement, Cate set down the pen. "Thank you for coming in."

By the time the third candidate sat opposite her, Cate's expectations for the level of professionalism from the candidates changed drastically. Mayor Sam and Nell's daughter Adeline, or Addie as her friends called her, grew up on Gull Island. Like Cate, she knew it like the back of her hand. Cate marveled at how knowledgeable Addie was about the latest trends in hospitality. She certainly did her homework. It appeared as if Addie was a shoo-in for the position when Cate asked her final question.

"Thinking about your current job as a bank teller, what has been your greatest weakness?" Cate leaned in, being sure to hear the response.

Addie paused for a moment. "I'm horrible with numbers, but I never forget a face." She bit her lip.

That sounded like a good trade-off to Cate. "You're hired. When can you start?"

****

After dropping off Jackson at the beach house, Knox swung by Bait & Switch. Business as usual on a Saturday with new vacationers stocking up on sunscreen and basic pantry supplies. With all-hands-on-deck, he comfortably headed home.

Detecting no sign of visitors at the house, Knox eased into the driveway. Uncle Charlie preferred to be left alone for his afternoon nap, mumbling his frustrations more than once. "I see no point in having someone monitor a grown man sleeping."

Inside the house, the television was off. Only the sound of the air-conditioning kicking in and loud snoring echoed down the hallway. As with a sleeping baby, he didn't risk waking his uncle prematurely. With a soft step, he entered the kitchen. The refrigerator was stocked with meal options prepared by caring hands. He removed a shepherd's pie and placed it on the countertop, allowing it to come to room temperature. He preheated the oven and set the table for two.

"Knox, are you stomping around?" yelled Uncle Charlie from his bedroom. "Time for the evening news."

"Right on schedule," shouted Knox. "Here I come."

One morning over breakfast, his uncle shared how difficult living alone was after Aunt Caroline passed away. "To have a sense of purpose, I made myself a daily schedule and have stuck to it ever since."

This was one of the many things Knox admired about him. Rather than wallow in his sadness, he chose to make the best of his circumstances by moving forward. As Knox entered the bedroom and caught sight of him, he couldn't help but think how much he would miss Uncle Charlie when he left.

Knox seated Uncle Charlie in his favorite recliner with a fresh glass of iced tea and a bowl of boiled peanuts, switching on the television with the volume at its loudest level. "I'm going to pop dinner in the oven and prepare a salad. Call me if you need me."

"Mm-hmm," his uncle grunted.

After Knox set the timer on the stove and chopped the salad, he joined his uncle on the couch. Charlie was laser focused on whatever the cable news anchor said, so Knox didn't try to strike up a conversation. Instead, he used the time to catch up on his emails and check social media. When dinner was ready, Knox carefully seated his uncle at the table. He broke the ice, focusing on the ins and outs of Charlie's day. "What did your father have to say when he called? Did he talk you into taking the job?" he grilled him, holding a forkful of salad midway to his mouth.

So much for easing into the conversation, Knox groaned inwardly. He placed his utensils in the three o'clock position on his plate. "Not exactly, but I suspect you already know that. Uncle Charlie, were you in on the plan to get me to come back to Gull Island?"

Uncle Charlie twitched his lips, placing the forkful of greens back on his plate. "Define plan."

Knox groaned. "Did you really need *me* here?"

"Need is a strong word. I certainly could use the help, but that's not what you're asking. Knox, you belong here as much as I do, maybe even more."

The words were spoken again…'you belong here,' and Knox experienced the same feeling as before—a sense of purpose. Time to shake it off. Too much was riding on his future to get caught up in this game his family was playing. "But I have this once-in-a-lifetime opportunity. I can't throw something like this away. I've worked too hard," he argued adamantly.

"Well then, I guess you've made your decision. When do you plan to leave?" His uncle clasped his hands together, resting his elbows on the table.

"C'mon, you need to eat. I can see in your cheekbones you've lost weight. I need to fatten you up before I take off. Listen, Uncle Charlie. I don't even know if I'm going to get the job. Let's concentrate on getting you better for the time being," he reasoned.

"When I met your aunt, I knew I'd marry her one day," Uncle Charlie began. "The way she smiled at me with love and respect in her eyes for the man I was, faults and all, made me want to be a better person. All I ever wanted to do was grow old with her."

"And why are you telling me this now?" Knox leaned back in his chair.

"I see how Cate smiles at you, and it reminds me of my Caroline. I don't want you to miss out on what could be the best thing in your life."

The quiet humming of the refrigerator filled the room. Neither of them uttered a word.

When Knox noticed Uncle Charlie yawning, he got up and cleared the table. He loaded the dishwasher with the dirty dishes and wiped down the kitchen table with a damp cloth.

"Help me to my recliner, please," begged Uncle Charlie.

"Absolutely." Knox hoisted his uncle out of the chair, guiding him slowly across the room. "How was your visit with Eliza's mother?"

"We shared stories about you, Eliza, Will, and Cate while eating a sliver of the chocolate cake she baked." Uncle Charlie rubbed his eyes.

"Our little foursome had a knack for finding trouble, especially in Eliza's mom's kitchen. Somehow, we managed to get in a squabble when baking some chocolate chip cookies. None of us would confess to how an entire bag of flour made its way all over the countertops and kitchen floor." Knox laughed at the memory.

The doorbell chimed, interrupting their conversation.

"Probably Will. He and I are riding over to the marina together to take a sunset cruise on Mayor Sam and Nell's boat. We're stopping by a few of the Purdey & Son projects beforehand so he can show me what makes them so unique. Are you sure you'll be okay for a few hours?" Knox paused a moment before aiming for the door.

"Henry's wife wants him to fix some shelves, so I expect he'll be stopping by again sometime soon. You'd think she'd figure out by now Henry is the last person you'd want swinging a hammer." He shook his head.

They both laughed.

"What did I miss?" Will asked as Knox let him in the door.

"Ol' Man Henry and a hammer. Need I say more?" Knox lifted his hands in the air.

Will laughed right along with them.

Knox excused himself and quickly showered, while Will kept Uncle Charlie company. Within ten minutes, he was ready to leave. Coming down the hallway toward the living room, he overheard Will. "I think he's leaving." He rounded the corner just in time to see Uncle Charlie drumming his fingers on the arm of the recliner. Knox drew in a deep breath and continued walking. "All set," he declared, and out the door he and Will strode. Knox silently wrestled with the tug on his heart, nudging him toward the future of his dreams.

****

From the cabinet behind the desk in her office, Cate grabbed a manila folder. After labeling it with Adeline's name, she slipped the new hire's resume inside. In the managerial binder, she flipped to the section on new employees in search of the payroll forms. Once she found what she was searching for, she made two copies—one for Adeline and another to keep handy. She adhered a yellow sticky note on Adeline's to remind herself to email the completed forms to the payroll department. Satisfied she had what she needed, she replaced the binder back to its rightful position on the bookshelf.

"How soon until she's ready to sub for me?" Eliza teased her. "I hear Charleston calling my name."

"Depends on how long it takes for you to train her," Cate playfully jabbed back. "Seriously, she is going to fit right in. I wouldn't be surprised if she's up to speed within a couple of weeks. The hardest part will be learning the computer system. The good thing is the software is user-friendly."

"Speaking of the word friendly, do you think you'll be able to play nice with Knox tonight? I hear the boat is a looker, but there won't be any place for you to hide."

"I will be on my best behavior." Cate powered down her computer and tidied up the desk.

"Any chance you can swing by my house and pick me up? Not too far out of your way, right?" Eliza arched an eyebrow.

"If you take the reservation book and packets to Bait & Switch, then yes," Cate replied. "I'd like to catch up with Jackson and see how he finished at the swim meet." She eyeballed her watch. "He should be home by now."

Eliza grabbed the clear basket bin with the packets, balancing it on a hip, and then swiped the book off the counter. "Text me when you leave, please." With her elbow, she clicked off the overhead lights.

"Get going." Cate insisted. "I'll lock up."

A group of teenagers was seated at the entryway of the building with ice cream cones in hand. Cate locked the front door behind her and weaved her way in and out of the late-day snackers to get to her cart.

At home, the front door was ajar. Jackson had a tendency to forget it required an extra nudge to firmly close. Cate mounted the stairs two at a time to give herself a mini-stretch. She hadn't the time to exercise all day.

Cate found Jackson sitting cross-legged on the kitchen counter focused on some cooking video playing on his phone. "Hello, there."

He glanced up and nodded, continuing with what sounded like a lesson on grilling steaks.

"How did it go today? I'm sorry I didn't get a chance to check Meet Mobile. I was swamped at work with the interviews and check-ins." Cate yanked open the refrigerator door and helped herself to a cold lime seltzer.

Jackson paused his video. "The morning dragged on. I didn't make the top ten in any of my events, which means I won't be going to the finals. So, if you need to find me this summer, I'll either be at work or hanging out with my friends at the beach, maybe crabbing."

Cate detected an underlying tone of happiness, not

disappointment, from Jackson concerning the results of today's meet. Something was not adding up.

"Um, Cate. Do you have a minute?" He slid off the counter and stood tall.

She satisfied her thirst with a long swig of seltzer to prepare for the incoming news.

"I told Knox today I don't want to swim in college." He drew his lower lip between his teeth. "I want to go to culinary school. He said I should tell you. So, I'm telling you. I hope you're not mad."

"Seriously, Jackson. You need to work on your delivery. Butter me up first, then hit me with your news," she sassed him.

"Does this mean you're mad? Knox said I should just be honest with you," he pleaded.

"Oh, did he?" Cate seethed.

"Should I have not mentioned that?" He scratched his head.

She set the can of seltzer on the counter and placed a hand on his arm. "I want you to be happy. Plain and simple. If that means you're going to culinary school instead of swimming in college, then so be it. You need to follow your dreams, not mine or Mom's or Dad's. Do what makes you happy, Jackson."

He let out a sizable breath. "Thanks, sis. Knox assured me you wouldn't be mad."

Cate grinned. "And, he's 100 percent right. I'm proud of you for staying true to who you are. Not everyone has the courage to speak his mind like you do." She stepped up on her tippy toes and kissed him on the cheek. "Plus, you're the best cook in the family. This doesn't come as a total surprise. I need to get dressed and on the road in ten minutes flat. Let's talk more later. A boat is calling my name."

In her borrowed dressing room, Cate changed out of her work clothes and slipped into a summery peach mini-dress and neutral-colored thong sandals that she laid out early this morning on the chaise in Grammy's bedroom. While washing her face, she debated if she should share with her brother what happened last night with Knox. If Jackson already knew, he would have mentioned it, she was sure. The part she was struggling with was Knox's insistence that her brother come clean with her. Do as I say and not as I do. To be fair, Cate appreciated his willingness to give Jackson a little nudge in the right direction. If only he had done the same with her and revealed his truth.

****

Knox and Will set off for the marina early, intending to make frequent stops. The best way for Knox to better understand the kind of projects Purdey & Son designed was to visit the works in progress. Having already acquainted himself with the types of structures they built, he now wanted to view them from the ground up. "I've taken the chance to check out your website and Internet presence. I've come up with a marketing proposal I'd like to present to you and your dad. The thirtysomethings are a whole audience you're not reaching. What you're doing with your projects fits within their core values. I'd like to show you how to rebrand yourself to tap into the demographic."

"My dad and I are anxious to hear your recommendations. Were you able to incorporate the eco-friendly side of the business—like landscape sustainability, energy efficiency, and healthy homes into your vision?"

"Being at the forefront of these trends will set your company apart from the others. I predict you'll see an uptick in nature-inspired projects and the use of repurposed materials, as well as requests for improved efficiency. This truly is an exciting time for your business," Knox commented.

"I wish you were sticking around. What Cate said last night had a hint of truth in it. My dad and I *would* benefit from having someone like you in the company. Purdey & Price has a nice ring, too." He poked him in the ribs with an elbow.

Knox could tell his best friend was putting the squeeze on him to stay, almost as hard as Uncle Charlie. He must admit, Purdey & Price sounded good. Plus, his love of nature combined with marketing intrigued him.

"Have you spoken to Eliza?" asked Knox, with his gaze glued on the road.

"If you're asking if Cate will be there, the answer is yes. According to what Eliza told me, Cate wouldn't want to disappoint Mayor Sam and Nell by being a no-show. Maybe you could shoot her a text. Tell her you can't wait to see her. It wouldn't hurt."

Knox relaxed a little. "Good idea. The last thing I want to do is scare her away. I've friends who have weathered long-distance relationships. You and Eliza, for example." His only roadblock was Cate. He had to break through and convince her to give their relationship another chance. They both deserved to have it all. Cate's dream of becoming a manager came true. Knox wanted the same thing, except in a different state. Why couldn't she see it this way? "Where are we headed?"

Will rolled up to a stop sign behind a few cars and carts. "Once traffic dies down a little, I think we'll be able to visit four of our newest work sites. Each house is a complete gut, down to the bare bones. The process is complicated in the sense we have to determine what works best within the natural landscape of the property. It also has to be functionally and aesthetically appealing. Next, we ask the clients for a wish list. Nothing is off-limits. This gives us a good peek into their headspace. From there, we whittle it down to their non-negotiables."

"What's a typical budget for these renovations?" Knox inquired.

"That's a tricky question. It can range from as little as 100K to as much as a couple million and more. Unlike when we were kids, these vacation homes are redesigned with the intent of becoming luxurious beach getaways. No more beach bungalows around here."

"Crazy how this island has changed," noted Knox, taking in the scenery.

"I know, right? What started as a small construction company is evolving into a multi-million-dollar business. If you were to join us, I think you'd be instrumental in the initial design phase, keeping the island intact while beautifying these magnificent homes. You are up on the newest trends in the eco-friendly side of construction. You also know how to market to the right audience," Will emphasized. Driving into a crushed oyster shell driveway, Will parked the truck in front of a skeletal frame of a house.

Knox followed his lead, getting out and walking toward the site.

"This house site is my favorite because it backs up

to the marsh. The owners wanted the view of the marsh to be the focal point of the house. How beautiful is this lot?"

Knox inhaled the familiar smell of pluff mud—the salty air of the Lowcountry. It never got old. Something about this particular lot spoke to him. For some reason, he imagined himself here, with Cate. "Wanted?" Knox scrunched up his face.

"Yeah, they withdrew their offer. This is now our spec house. Rebuilding it from the ground up. Stick around and this project could be your baby."

Knox did a double-take. "Seriously? I'm leaving in a month to start my next adventure."

"Maybe the next adventure is here with Cate." Will shrugged.

"I care about Cate," Knox stated with conviction. "I've always had a thing for her, but I…I can't stay here on Gull Island. I'm sorry, Will."

"Suit yourself. This piece of property has potential from a professional standpoint and personal. I recall a conversation between the four of us about raising our kids together. Sure is a shame you don't want to put down roots in a place you used to call home."

The disappointment in his best friend's voice pained him to hear. Knox wanted to check off the boxes in both his professional career and personal life, but as it stood, they weren't aligned. First step would involve getting Cate to agree to a long-distance relationship. Then maybe one day, he'd return to Gull Island. For now, having it all didn't include living on Gull Island.

The two friends climbed back into the truck and visited three additional sites. "Will, I'm in awe of what Purdey & Son has accomplished here," exclaimed

Knox. "So much has changed since I lived on the island." He was relieved Will stopped strong-arming him to stay. If Will so easily came to terms with his leaving, maybe Cate would, too.

"We better get moving." Knox glanced at his phone. "We literally don't want to miss the boat."

****

From a distance, Cate observed Will's truck screeching into the marina's parking lot. She wasn't surprised they were cutting it close. On the way over, Eliza filled her in on their quick side trip to the latest Purdey & Son's projects on the island—Will's last attempt to convince Knox to stay. By dangling the prospect of joining the company in front of him, Will hoped Knox might be tempted to change his mind. As of the morning, Knox was leaning toward taking the job, if offered. Cate chuckled, witnessing Knox and Will scrambling to board the boat before it left the dock. After all these years, she and Knox traded places. Cate was right on time.

Thinking back to last night, Cate's hopes for the lighthouse tour had been high, especially her romantic hopes for the two of them deepening their relationship. But that didn't happen, or at least not on his end. Like it or not, she'd have to come to terms with his leaving. What that meant for their relationship was yet to be determined. It certainly would make it a lot harder. On the bright side, at least he texted her a little while ago. She decided to live in the moment and enjoy what time she did have left with Knox. If a long-distance relationship was in her future, she'd deal with it then.

Chapter Sixteen

Knox hustled with Will by his side to the finger piers where the vessel was docked. He barely made it in time for Mayor Sam to grant them permission to come aboard. Knox and Will said their hellos and oohed and aahed over the couple's newly acquired craft and its state-of-the-art features, like the dual-console and expansive sun lounge. In the Lowcountry, boats were as important as cars, if not more. The best way to experience the island was by sea.

The boat ride got underway. Knox's interest was piqued when Mayor Sam shared seaworthy tidbits from the captain's chair. Cruising to the area where dolphins congregate, Knox observed Mayor Sam cut the engine in order to drift for a short time.

The men relocated to the sun lounge where Nell, Eliza, and Cate were busy chatting about the lighthouse's transformation.

Knox barely had time to sit before Mayor Sam got down to business. "Thank you for joining us tonight. You four are the future of Gull Island. Great things are happening here. With Purdey & Sons transforming Gull Island into a place people want to call home and Guest Services making the island a vacation destination like none other. Mark my words—Gull Island is changing for the better."

Knox nodded.

"Please help yourselves to the light spread my beautiful wife has prepared," Mayor Sam continued. "There are beverages in the cooler and dessert for later. Don't be shy."

Knox admired the platters of food occupying a makeshift table fully dressed with a solid red tablecloth, impressed by Nell's smart idea to place a large conch shell on top of the cocktail napkins to keep them from blowing away. From the corner of his eye, he spied Cate and Eliza helping themselves to a light sampling of deviled eggs, grape jelly meatballs, and ham sliders.

"I'm glad to see the four of you together again," Nell commented while dishing a few meatballs onto her plate.

The light wind carried the conversation, enabling Knox to eavesdrop.

"Just like old times." Cate played it off perfectly. She popped a deviled egg in her mouth, hindering her from saying more.

Knox took advantage of Nell's proximity, slipping next to Cate, lightly placing his hand on the small of her back. He sensed her stiffening slightly, keeping herself in check. By then, everyone congregated around the table, sampling the bounty of food. The time to speak with her in private passed.

"Have you heard the good news?" Nell clasped her hands.

Knox dropped his arm to his side. "What news?"

"Cate hired Adeline to fill her open position." She puffed out her chest.

"Congratulations. Adeline is a real people person. This job is right up her alley." He bent over to swipe a ham sandwich from the table, stepping aside to allow

Mayor Sam to join them.

Once the group was settled in their seats, Mayor Sam began. "Thank you again, Will, for spearheading the scavenger hunt for the third year in a row. Not only has it made the community and outside visitors to the island come together, but it has also raised valuable funds for the Lowcountry Conservation Fund. Involved citizens like you have made my job as Mayor a pleasure. But, after much reflection, I have decided not to run for re-election."

Knox witnessed Cate subtly tap Eliza on the leg. The group previously discussed at length whether or not he would run again. He held the position for over ten years. Plenty of rumors swirled around town, especially at Bait & Switch and the post office. Tongues were flapping with speculation as to who might fill his shoes. Knox recalled Cate voicing her opinion about Gull Island needing a fresh, younger face. "You'll be greatly missed." Knox verbalized what the group was thinking.

"I appreciate you saying that, but I've been considering a certain someone who is active in the community…"

A buzzing sound cut off the mayor mid-sentence. Everyone searched for the source.

Knox dug deep into his pocket and quickly whipped out his phone. He glanced at the number displayed on the screen, his stomach clamping. "Please excuse me. I need to take this call."

****

The size of the boat didn't lend itself to privacy. From the snippets of conversation Cate overheard, Knox was offered the position, but she didn't catch whether or not he accepted. She noted Mayor Sam and

Nell whispering between themselves. As much as she wanted to fill them in, she opted not to share his business. She was more interested in eavesdropping on Knox's conversation. Like it or not, the result of the call impacted her future.

Knox rejoined the group with beads of perspiration on his forehead. Cate silently hoped he would be honest with his explanation. She had a hunch the news would not be well received by Mayor Sam and Nell.

"I apologize for interrupting your announcement," Knox began, standing front and center for all to hear.

"It seems my news is not the hot topic tonight. Young man, do you have something you wish to share?" Mayor Sam folded his hands, resting them on his ample belly.

"No sense avoiding the truth. I received a job offer with the National Wildlife Preservation in Washington, D.C. as a staff photographer."

Cate observed Mayor Sam and Nell exchange a furtive glance, bewildered by the news.

"I'm assuming congratulations are in order. You accepted the position?" Mayor Sam asked politely.

Nell discreetly grabbed hold of his hand.

Cate noticeably inhaled, waiting for him to break her heart…again. As if Knox could read her mind, he stared into Cate's eyes.

"I did not," he simply said.

Relief washing over her, Cate exhaled.

"I have until tomorrow to decide," he muttered in a monotone voice.

Cate slumped her shoulders, mirrored by Eliza and Will. Her gut reaction was right, despite Knox's best intentions; he wasn't willing to pass up the next best thing.

"You'll make the right decision," Nell declared with a forced smile.

Cate wasn't so sure.

A pod of dolphins suddenly sprang up near the boat, gliding in and out of the calm water. The splashing sea mammals were a welcome distraction from Knox's unsettling news. Cate leaned over the side to catch a glimpse when the calves broke the surface for air. Frolicking near the boat, the pod soon lost interest and vanished as swiftly as it appeared.

Cate overheard Sam grilling Knox on the particulars of the job, asking questions while simultaneously offering unsolicited advice. Her interest in the details waned, resigned to the inevitable demise of their relationship.

When the sun began its final descent, Mayor Sam resumed his position in the captain's chair, revving the engine for the boat's return to the marina.

Cate noticed the vibrant streaks of reds and yellows painted in the sky, announcing the arrival of the crescent moon. She remained quiet, spending the final minutes on the boat taking in the glorious view. Before the boat docked, Cate cozied up to Nell. "Mayor Sam never finished his announcement," she whispered.

"He's running for the open state representative position," Nell replied in a quiet voice, her face beamed with pride. "I'll take care of the rest." She scooted Cate away. "Go enjoy the remainder of the boat ride with your friends."

When the boat docked, Cate and the others exchanged thank yous and hugs, along with promises to Mayor Sam to brainstorm on a potential mayoral replacement.

Nell asked to have a word with Knox, causing him to lag behind as the others crossed the short space to the dock.

Cate secretly hoped their conversation had something to do with her. Better yet, maybe Nell was attempting to sell him on the idea of staying on Gull Island permanently. Cate had experienced firsthand how persuasive Nell could be. Cate lingered, wishing Nell would call her over. Two were better than one, especially in this instance. When Mayor Sam approached, asking if Cate was ready to go, she realized the conversation was not for her ears.

By that time, Eliza and Will paired off, leaving Cate to drive herself home. Aiming her steps toward the parking lot, she replayed the phone call on the boat in her mind, willing herself to remember any minute detail indicating if Knox planned to take the job. Cate reasoned he could be biding time to let the potential employer down easy. Then again, maybe she was the one he intended to disappoint.

"Cate," hollered Knox from behind, his deep voice carrying with the summer breeze.

She stopped short, debating if she ought to have this conversation tonight. She needed to be prepared for whatever the outcome, not rely on her emotions to speak her truth. Her brief moment of indecision gave Knox time to catch up. Biting her lip, she faced him. "My car is parked over by the entrance. Need a ride home?"

"Please," he answered, quickening his steps.

Together they ambled in the direction of her car, their steps in sync again.

Cate engaged him in small talk about the dolphins and the picture-perfect sunset, careful to avoid discussing his job offer, putting off the inevitable for a little bit longer. Even now, his close proximity caused her heart to stir and her breath to catch.

"Your managerial position opens new doors of opportunity in the company. How far up the corporate ladder will you climb?"

"That's the least of my concerns." Cate stopped and turned to face him, her words purposeful and direct. "The new and improved version of me is experiencing each moment, one at a time. I'm no longer worried about situations beyond my control. Being present is my new mantra."

"Does your vision board reflect your new attitude?" He tilted his head.

"I'm surprised you remembered I keep one." Her mouth twitched.

He inched closer. "There are lots of things I remember."

"As a matter of fact, it does. Work life balance is what I'm aiming for," she declared, "wherever that leads me." Cate clicked the key fob, unlocking the car. Thinking back to when they were a couple, she recalled how Knox typically drove. "Not tonight," she murmured, barely above a whisper. Cate climbed into the driver's seat, firmly in control.

Knox crossed in front of the car and sat in the passenger's seat. Buckling up, he kept a steady gaze on her.

She inserted the key into the ignition and shifted into drive.

"How about we stop by the inlet?" he proposed.

"No, I have a better idea," Cate countered. In fewer than five minutes, she eased the car into the exact same spot where their previous relationship ended, the pier, unusually devoid of summertime visitors for that time of night.

"Let's go sit under the moonlight," he suggested.

Cate nodded, unable to verbalize her emotions. She owed it to herself to hear him out before deciding which path she'd take, hopeful for a better ending. Her mind drifted to Grammy, the person she relied on for comfort when life didn't go her way. Somehow, Grammy was with her in spirit. A sense of calm suddenly came over her, triggering a willingness to accept her fate with Knox despite how painful it might be.

The brightness of the moon shone down on the end of the pier like a spotlight on a stage. Cate sat with Knox on opposite ends of a vacant bench, listening to the water lapping up against the pilings, not ready to speak. Cate lifted her chin, pretending to stare at the stars. Right here, right now, she wanted to give him a chance to explain himself.

"When my father floated the idea of me coming to Gull Island to help Uncle Charlie, I was worried about bumping into you. The way I left things wasn't right. I should've been honest and told you my feelings. Instead I chose the easy way out by breaking up. You're long overdue for an apology. I'm sorry I hurt you, Cate." He raked his fingers through his hair.

Cate breathed in the salty air, keeping herself quiet for a little while longer.

"And then on my very first day on the island, there you were at Bait & Switch, beautiful as ever. I convinced myself to keep my distance, but that didn't work well. Every time we bumped into each other, I wanted more. You're an amazing person, Cate. You're independent. Self-confident. *On time,*" he uttered in disbelief.

Cate couldn't help but laugh. "Yes, I am. I've finally figured out who I am and what I want from life. I've learned not to be so concerned about what might happen that I miss out on the here and now. Like loving my new job and being surrounded by family and friends."

Knox drew in a long breath, rubbing a hand over the sandy-blond stubble on his jaw. "Do you think you can make room for me in your life?"

"That depends." She turned to face him, her breaths quickening. "What about your new job?" She couldn't wait any longer. She needed the answer, whatever it might be.

"When I got the offer, all I could think about was you," he confessed.

"Why?" Cate blurted, her heart skipping a beat.

He swallowed hard. "For the last couple of years, I've been running from place to place in search of the next best thing. It took me coming back home to Gull Island to figure out what was missing. You. You are what's missing." He caressed her cheek.

Cate straightened her spine. "How can you be so sure?" she pleaded.

"Gull Island is where I belong, with you, my uncle, and my friends. I can't go back and change the past, Cate, but I can commit to my future. I'm not moving to D.C. for a job." His lips curled upward.

"But, how will you make a living?" Cate drew near, no longer able to keep still.

"I'm pretty sure Uncle Charlie could use an extra set of hands at Bait & Switch. Plus, I'm constantly getting pinged about freelance opportunities."

"What about Purdey & Son?" Cate implored, her happiness growing inside.

He chuckled. "Also, a consideration. Will and his dad are expanding their business day by day. I'd like to see how I might fit into their plan."

"Does this mean you're sticking around for good?" She squeezed his knee.

He gently lifted Cate to her feet, folding her into his warm embrace, kissing her tenderly…once, then twice. He pressed his forehead against hers, his focus mirroring the stillness of the night. "Does that answer your question?" he whispered.

Cate felt her knees go weak, completely lost in the deep blue eyes of the man standing in front of her and speaking his truth. "Why, yes. I believe it does. Welcome home, Knox. Welcome home."

A word about the author...

Jennifer Vido is a sweet romance author with a love for all things cozy. An avid booklover, she pens the Jen's Jewels author interview column on FreshFiction.com. As an Arthritis Foundation advocate, she has been featured by Lifetime Television, Redbook, The New York Times, The Baltimore Sun, and Arthritis Today. Currently, she lives with her husband in the Baltimore area with two rescue dogs and a rescue cat, and she is the proud parent of two sons. For more information, please visit her website http://www.jennifervido.com.

Thank you for purchasing
this publication of The Wild Rose Press, Inc.

For questions or more information
contact us at
info@thewildrosepress.com.

The Wild Rose Press, Inc.
www.thewildrosepress.com